VALOR

ROHAN YATHISH
VISHAL YATHISH

TABLE OF CONTENTS

Prologue 1

1. The Forest 3
2. The Noble Art of Bounty Hunting 9
3. A Scene of Power 16
4. In the Sad Excuse for a Rebellion 23
5. Rellicos City 30
6. Trading Blows 35
7. The Dark Mage 40
8. Wayloc 46
9. The Demon Dog and the Corrupted Cat 51
10. Master of Malice 59
11. Lore 65
12. All in Favor of Dying..69
13. Fallen Magic 73
14. Mendelo's Request 76
15. The Throne of Fear 80
16. The Rain 84
17. Past and Present..87
18. Finally, a Real Rebellion 91
19. Siege 94
20. The Rebellion's Last Stand 97
21. The Shadow Colossus 101
22. The End and the Beginning......................................104

PROLOGUE

IT WAS MANY CENTURIES AGO when life on earth was mostly eradicated. The world was blissfully ignorant in the summer of 2201, unaware of its impending doom. Around the world, things were warming up and not just because it was June. Billions of miles away, the sun was growing hotter than ever before. Its boiling surface bubbled and occasionally, ejected large splashes of itself out into the solar system. It radiated heat three times as much as usual. Then, without any warning, it spat a massive surge of fire into the solar system.

After devouring Mercury, ravaging Venus, cracking the moon, and sending so much debris into Earth's orbit that it almost had rings like Saturn, the fire wave got to our planet. Barely anybody noticed the massive firewall in the sky heading straight toward them. It was, after all, 2201, when 99% of the population had phones implanted into their faces, though everyone was sweating profusely with the intense heat. The part of the population whose sight wasn't clouded with things like Mega Robot Mutant Alien Slayerz 2 could not see anything past the huge clouds of smoke fumes covering the sky. Factories were almost as common as phones and polluted the air with dirtier versions of clouds.

So, just as all life was being enveloped by fire, no one could have thought less about it. This event was later known as the Remaking. There were some surviving humans, however, who were lucky to be in bunkers or in the ocean. And those few would never know why the sun acted like a baby and threw a temper tantrum (or should I say, a *temperature* tantrum).

From then on, life was never the same. Buildings collapsed to make way for lush jungles, deserts, mountains, lakes, and more. New and diverse plants and animals thrived. Under the new circumstances, it took a millennium to regrow life that had any distinct intelligence.

Humanity returned from those few survivors. They settled down in new places and adapted. Information was passed down from them, which was lucky, otherwise humanity would not be very smart. But this time, humans were side by side with monsters and creatures of their own intelligence. They used relics of the past, such as intact books, to name these creatures. For example, when they discovered a sub-species of human living in the mountains that had adapted pointy ears, they named them "elves."

With the earth wiped clean of all that history, humans started anew and built their society with those they respected. Alongside elves and similar creatures, they created cities and planted trees. And, as is common with all intelligent creatures, they waged war.

Chaos reigned for a long time afterward. Under all the calamity and violence, an evil tyrant easily stepped up to take control of everything. And under the name the Magistrate, a rule of cruelty and terror like the world had never seen began.

Only a few rebellions sparked and were put out just as quickly by the Magistrate's servants. Now, in the year 3411, it seems hopeless to fight back. Will bravery prevail at last?

Will anyone have the courage to stand up to the Magistrate once and for all?

1

THE FOREST

THUNK!

A furry winter boot slammed onto the icy ground of a dark forest. A figure walked across the cold land. In the distance, a faint orange light peeked through the trees. The figure was cautious. It was a dangerous time, so it was best to be on guard.

The light grew brighter and brighter as the figure got closer and closer. *Just a bit further*, thought the figure. The light danced across the hard, icy leaves. The figure pulled out something short and shiny, and with a slash, the large frozen branch in front of the figure crashed to the ground, shattering into millions of pieces of frozen wood.

The figure stepped out of the wood and was no longer shadowed by the towering trees. It wore a furry winter coat with a hood that shadowed a mask covering the figure's face. The visor glared in the light that came from an old cabin twenty feet away made of old wood and glass. There was an ancient sign stuck into the earth, slightly lopsided, imprinted with faded letters. *Lianthorn's Shop of Magical Weaponry and Items.*

With a loud creak, the door swung open. Around the cabin, there were all sorts of things on the shelves of what looked like a store. Swords, shields, bottles, and other things sat on the wooden shelves. A desk stood at the back of the room before a chair holding a tall, old, slightly chubby man with glasses, pointy ears, oily gray hair, a brown shirt with yellow overalls, and shiny black shoes. He also had many wrinkles, was fast asleep, and his head rested on the desk in a puddle of drool that dripped down onto the floor.

The figure rang the bell on the desk. The elf continued to drool. The figure tapped the elf's head rather hard. The elf shuddered and rolled over. The figure held up the knife that cut down that branch and banged the flat side against the elf's forehead.

"I'M AWAKE! I'm awake..."

He had a high voice, a bit like a mouse. The elf jolted up, eyes wide. His yellow pupils swung onto the figure.

"What did you do that for?" asked the elf.

"Hey there, Lian," said the figure, ignoring the elf's question.

The elf put his head back down and groaned.

"A few more minutes, please. It's been busy in the shop today."

"You have the rest of the night to nap," said the figure, taking off the full-face mask and removing the hood. She was a woman who had long, dark hair and grayish blue eyes. "Now, get up."

"Fine... *FINE*..." Lian whined. "I'm up..."

Lian raised his head a few inches, his eyes dazed.

"What do you want today, Veronica? May I interest you in some potions? Maybe some snow gear? Just pick, please, I'd like to get back to... very important business..."

"Mhm. I'm sure. Now, one sand eye potion, grade, a double-bladed sword," listed the person named Veronica, counting on her fingers. "some desert gear, and a force-grade rellicos pistol. Sooner, rather than later if you please."

Lian raised his right eyebrow, now almost completely over his groggy nature, a look of interest on his face. "So, you're bounty hunting in the desert, now?"

Veronica looked at him curiously. He was dumping the contents of several different colored bottles into a large ceramic bowl, the yellow substance inside bubbling and steaming. One of the sizzling yellow bubbles burst, temporarily engulfing Lian's hand. He gave a small jerk and shook the liquid off.

"Yes," Veronica said matter-of-factly.

Lian's face suddenly became stern. "And how much are they paying you this time, hm?"

Veronica knew where he was getting to.

"Three thousand one hundred fifty-seven reliccas. When I capture the victim and give him to the employer, I'm going to buy myself something nice, maybe a robot. I heard that's the new craze in Rellicos City." She hesitated, then continued. "The employer works for the Magistrate."

"What in the—" cried Lian.

"I'm not proud of it. I'm not."

She really wasn't. The Magistrate was, in her opinion, evil. Every story about tyrants abusing their power was brought to life by him. Veronica heard of the imprisonment. It was well known that anyone who stood up to him was put in jail immediately. But she was willing to get money from anyone, even evil people. The problem was, like most of the world, she didn't know just how evil he was.

"But he works for the *Magistrate*," Lian hissed indignantly. He was dropping some more ingredients into the potion but timidly. "How can you do that? How can anyone do that." The potion stopped bubbling. Veronica saw this.

"Well, if the potion's done…"

Lian wore a scowl as big as his overalls, but he got a bottle and filled it with the now sand-colored potion. Then, without talking, he put the bottle and a small gun that was intricately painted blue and gray onto the table. After that, he rummaged underneath his desk to find a long sword with two blades on each side and thrust it into Veronica's hands.

"Good day to you."

Well, Veronica thought, *if Lian was going to be like that, I have no business being here.* She then put the potion and gun in her pockets and carried the sword in her hands as she walked out the door.

Veronica was annoyed. Didn't Lian understand that good and evil don't matter if it's in the service of making money? Who cares what happened to the people the Magistrate captured if the rest of them survived? She had nothing to do with all the crime sprees, the suffering caused by the Magistrate. To take her mind off Lian, she examined her sword. It was extremely high-quality. The refined, sharp edges, the shiny, polished crest with its shimmering gems. Her target was going to have a hard time escaping.

The forest became darker as the moon drew lower and the trees became thicker. Veronica's cabin should only be a mile away. She recognized the tree next to her, an ancient, twisted one, to be near her cabin. Just in case, she drew out her old plasma rifle. It barely worked, but it was a better option than using her new pistol, as she didn't want to waste its energy.

The sky was slowly turning a dark shade of gray as the big, cracked, glowing orb in the sky was hidden by the trees above Veronica. It was so silent and dark she could hear the crickets chirping and the breeze gradually moving the snow. Her breathing and heartbeat felt loud compared to the quiet of the forest.

Veronica stopped walking, pulled off her backpack, and quickly rummaged through. A few seconds later, she grabbed a compass from her bag and swung it on her back. Northwest. If she was correct, she was one-fourth of a mile away from her cabin.

She continued to tread across the snow but slightly faster. The sooner Veronica reached her cabin, the better. She drew out her new sword.

Veronica walked through the maze of woods and hit a dead end. She turned and walked into a frigid clearing of snow. Through the trees in front of her, she could see the faint light of her cabin.

She was very tired. Veronica's heart was beating fast, and she was panting. The sky was almost a pure, inky black. Her heartbeat was growing louder. Or was it her heartbeat? It didn't sound like a heartbeat. And it was slower. The noise grew to a loud thumping, and it was coming from the trees. She saw a flash of transparent blue from within two shrubs, and Veronica knew what was making the sound.

From the snow-covered bush ran something icy blue. In the gaps between the trees beside her came four more blue blurs. They slowed down and moving closer, started circling Veronica. They looked like Dobermans, but instead of flesh and skin, crystals and ice covered their bodies, legs, heads, and tails. Their eyes glowed white, and their teeth were made of icicles. Two of the icehounds had tails that resembled that of scorpions and were pointed at Veronica. Two of them bared their fangs. The last and biggest one was around the size of a jaguar with teeth like a saber-toothed tiger. It seemed to be the leader of this group of icehounds.

Veronica met icehounds every other day and was completely used to almost all of them on Mount Vilgroth. So, when approached by this group of strays, she showed absolutely no fear whatsoever. Instead of attacking the group head on, Veronica stayed put.

The smallest of the group lunged, rather unwisely, at Veronica. This was its last mistake. Veronica, feet still firmly on the ground, grabbed the icehound's head in midair and smashed it to the ground face first. The icehounds head shattered. This was the other icehounds' cue to attack her. One of the icehounds ran at Veronica. The two icehounds with scorpion tails walked slowly toward Veronica, tail tips raised. She immediately raised her sword and stabbed the sprinting icehound in the chest, sending shards of crystal in the air. Veronica flicked it off her sword, throwing the limp, slightly cracked icehound at one of the scorpion-tailed ones. Both hounds dissolved into icy dust. The remaining scorpion-tail icehound jumped toward her, but Veronica drew out her gun and with a flash of blue light, blew the poor icehound to smithereens.

The remaining icehound, along with being the biggest and most intimidating of what used to be its group, was also, so it seemed, the smartest of the lot. Instead of lunging at Veronica, it sprinted in circles around her and lunged at her from behind. This caught Veronica off guard. The icehound tore at her backpack. Veronica turned around and tried to blast the creature with her plasma gun, but the icehound bit into it the second she fired. The gun was ripped out of Veronica's hands and twisted into a pretzel by the icehound, which only took a few seconds. Luckily, it was so distracted with destroying the gun, it didn't notice when Veronica slashed at it with her sword. The icehound noticed but just barely. The sword tip slashed its eye, sending it reeling in pain. The icehound backed away from Veronica quickly, growling. Then, it disappeared into the shadows.

Veronica waited for a minute or two, just in case there were more icehounds. Then, she kicked her now useless gun into the forest, picked up her backpack, crammed the stuff that had fallen out back into it, and walked toward her cabin.

2

THE NOBLE ART OF BOUNTY HUNTING

THE NEXT MORNING WAS CHAOTIC. Veronica rushed to fix every-thing in her house before meeting the employer. Her pet fire lizard went through three tubs during a bath. (It was tedious work, dumping melted metal cups into the woods.) She quickly changed into desert gear, which was basically Veronica's snow gear, except it was the color of sand, and it wasn't furry. She quickly drank a cup of water to replace breakfast. Then, she ran out the door, put on her mask, hopped on her plasma cycle (a type of motorcycle powered by plasma), and drove east.

It was a very steep ride down Mount Vilgroth and very bumpy, too. If not for her plasma cycle, she would have been one hour late to her meet-ing. Instead, she got there in around thirty minutes. Immediately down the east side of Mount Vilgroth was a massive desert. Veronica reached the bottom, which took around ten minutes, and sand flew onto her visor.

After twenty minutes of driving, Veronica saw a black dot in the distance, slightly blurred by the desert haze. *That should be him*, Veronica thought. She was right. When she came closer, the black dot became bigger and clearer. When Veronica got closer, the gray dot became a humanoid figure. It was a robot, which had no legs and floated in midair. Its singular eye was glowing blue.

"Hey!" Veronica called to the robot once she got close enough. The robot did not respond. Veronica drove closer and stopped in front of the robot, then dismounted her bike.

"By any chance, are you the employer?"

The robot spoke. It was a high, muffled, oddly distorted rasp of a voice, sort of like an old recording. In fact, Veronica suspected it *was* an old recording. "Indeed. You must be the hunter."

"Yes," replied Veronica.

"As you may know," the robot said, "I shall offer you three thousand one hundred fifty-seven reliccas for the capture of a man known as Terren Fallus."

The robot pulled out a small metal orb with a hole on top and a button on its right side. He pressed the button. Instantly, a hologram was projected through the hole, showing the face of a man with dark skin and hair with a short beard, whose eyes were not too far apart and whose nose was quite long. "He is wanted for breaking into the Rellicos City Weapons Vault. It is rumored Mr. Fallus here wanted to start a rebellion against the Magistrate. Your job is to find him and bring him to me, dead or alive." The robot paused for a moment and added, "Preferably alive."

"Underst—"

"Wait. I'm missing something..." interrupted the robot. "Ah, yes, the location. My sources tell me he is in the town of Madakal. That should be enough to send you off. Get him to me by sundown or no payment."

"Understood," said Veronica slowly, making sure that he wouldn't interrupt, and then hopped on her bike, checked her compass, and sped off east.

The ride was very long and very dull. Veronica was thinking of things that she could be doing if she hadn't taken this job when she saw something in the distance. It was hard to see, as the walls were almost the exact color as the sand below it. When Veronica got closer, however, she saw its unsaturated yellow contrast with the bright, cloudless sky above. The borderless town had many sandstone buildings. Some were towers and some were small houses. All along the road were merchants, bandits, elves, and noblemen.

He must be here, Veronica thought. She squinted through the crowd. When she couldn't find him, she got off her bike and walked through the mass of people, dragging her bike with her. Veronica still couldn't see Terren.

"Get out of the way!" she yelled through the crowd, which dispersed enough for her to see a woman with a large turban welcoming a long-nosed, dark-haired man she recognized as Terren Fallus into a tall house with a flat roof.

"Gotcha," Veronica muttered to herself. She pushed away a few bandits. She ran at the door of the house and pulled out her pistol. Veronica slowed down as she reached the house and raised her gun. There was an extremely loud *pew* sound and...

BOOM!

A giant hole was blasted through the door. Then, after a few seconds, it fell with a tremendous *bang*. Veronica looked at the woman in the turban, but she did not see Terren.

"Where is he?!" Veronica shouted at the woman in the turban.

"Hrm..." she murmured. She looked terrified.

"Did you hear me?!" Veronica asked threateningly. *"Where is he?"*

"Mrmm…" The woman was cowering. After a few seconds, she pointed up. Veronica looked where she pointed. There was a huge hole in the roof. Veronica put her gun in her pocket and pulled a large crow-bar-shaped tool from her bag. She grabbed one of the sides of the hole with the hook of the tool and pulled. The hook launched Veronica upward to the second floor. There was another hole in the roof of this floor. Veronica pulled upward onto the roof of the building, now slightly tired. Terren was turned the other way, looking across the sea of sand.

"Hey, there," Veronica said calmly. Terren gave a start and turned. "I assume you're Terren Fallus."

"You assume correctly." He talked slowly and his voice was deep and full of suspicion. He squinted at Veronica. "And you are?"

"Veronica Korix. You're coming with me."

Terren's suspicion seemed to fade away. He stopped squinting. "Ah, you're a hunter. You've come to take me to that Magistrate servant. What're you going to do with the money when you take me in?"

"That's my business, not yours. Now, as I said, you're coming with me," said Veronica.

"No, I don't think I will," said Terren. Veronica shrugged and advanced toward Terren, unsheathing her sword. Terren reacted with the speed of a cheetah and pulled out a big, golden blade. He pointed it directly at Veronica's face. Veronica stopped walking.

"I'm warning you…" Terren said quietly. Veronica put her hand to her gun holster and clutched the gun in it. They made eye contact for a few seconds. The air was very tense. Veronica quickly turned a dial on her gun to make sure it was on stun mode. Then, without warning, and to Terren's surprise, Veronica pulled out her gun and clenched the trigger. If not for Terren's reflexes, it was likely that he would have been knocked off the roof. He dodged the blast and pointed his shiny sword at Veronica, stroked the middle of the sword, and muttered something indistinct.

Hisssssss... Blam!

In a second, the middle of the sword opened, and out came a bolt of yellow lightning that grazed Veronica's shoulder and refracted off the floor, making yet another large hole in the roof.

"Oh, you're gonna pay for that!" exclaimed Veronica, rubbing her shoulder. She lunged at Terren, her sword high in the air. Terren held up his sword, and the swords collided with a tremendous *clang.* Terren pushed his sword, sending Veronica staggering backward. Veronica sprinted at Terren. Terren held out his sword, but Veronica surprised him by sliding to the floor. She swiftly got up behind Terren and slashed his back, sending him reeling forwards.

"Ahh... *Ahhhhh...*" Terren yelled as he clung to his back. He staggered and fell to the ground, then turned over. Veronica was pointing her sword directly between Terren's eyes. He was going cross-eyed trying to keep his eyes on the tip of the sword.

"Stand... down..." Veronica whispered just loud enough for Terren to hear. And, very slowly, Terren nodded.

The ride home was the same as the ride to the employer except it felt quicker. Ideas of what things she could buy with her money floated through her mind. In no time, she was at home.

Veronica felt a hot surge of anger. Lian was standing right before her door, his arms crossed and his face like stone. She approached Lian.

"Yes?" Veronica said it calmly, though she was furious.

"Suppose you got that money? Suppose you're going to head right out to Rellicos City tomorrow?" His expression did not change at all.

"Indeed," said Veronica coldly.

"Hope you like that new thing you're gonna get," Lian said coldly. He then turned and walked through the woods in the direction of his shop.

"What a bihk," Veronica muttered to herself. (Bihk means something in elvish that is, in general, quite rude.) She twisted the doorknob to her cabin and entered. As usual, her fire lizard was slowly melting its cage. Veronica took the fire lizard out of the cage by its tail and replaced the cage with one hand, the other still holding the lizard. Once the lizard was in a new, not melted cage, Veronica decided to take an early sleep. (She couldn't wait for the next day.)

But the next day did not come immediately.

Veronica was standing in a dark room with a door at the other end of it. She was walking slowly toward the door in a royal manner, her hands behind her back. Veronica twisted the doorknob with a gloved hand slightly hidden by a purple and black cloak. The room beyond this one was almost as dark as the one before except there was a lamp on the top that emitted a faint white light directly over what looked like a mound. The light was too faint to tell what it was.

Then, Veronica spoke—but not in her voice. A high, clear, raspy voice came out of her mouth. This was certainly not Veronica. "The Magistrate will see you in five days. Your powers will soon be his."

The thing moved, and the man saw that it was a man. He raised his head. It was Terren Fallus. He wore a ragged gray shirt and ragged gray pants, and he looked like he hadn't eaten for a day.

"The Magistrate will never win," he said. "There will be others who will fight."

"Au contraire, Mr. Fallus," the man sneered. "We have another target you might remember from the other day. Her powers will also soon belong to the Magistrate. By the start of the summer, the world will be reduced to nothing but fear and chaos. The world will become a world worthy of the Magistrate with me right beside him."

"You're mad," breathed Terren. "Mad, I tell you."

"Mad, yes. There is no denying that," said the man. "But most certainly powerful."

The man raised her gloved hand toward Terren, stroked the back of his wrist, and muttered, "Khrovini."

Instantly, Terren's body collided with a wall, a *cracking* noise punctured the air, and Veronica laughed. Then, she woke up. Her chest heaving, she fell back onto her bed and fell back to sleep. When she woke up, she wouldn't remember that night's dream.

3

A SCENE OF POWER

At 10:25 a.m., Veronica set out for Lian's shop, holding her lizard by the tail. The lizard flailed his arms playfully the whole time, his blood-red tongue sticking out. She arrived at 10:56 and handed the lizard to Lian, who was still sulky but took the lizard into his cabin anyway without a word.

Veronica went back to the cabin and hid all her valuables by 11:28. It was 11:30 when she finally headed out for Reliccos City, which she knew was south. Icehounds wouldn't dare attack her in broad daylight, and the most dangerous creatures apart from them were some feeble bambakambo. (Bambakambo are some peaceful mammals that only use their corrosive saliva in self-defense.)

It was oddly chilly and thus made the walk to the edge of the forest much longer than it should have been. Either that or the various interruptions. At 11:53, a family of bambakambo walked through the trail (Bambakambo look like small, dinosaur-headed monkeys. They have long legs with spikes on the ends of them instead of feet, two pairs of tiny arms, a scaly chest, a shell, and a short tail. The horns are stubby and are used for the storing of their acid spit. The sides of their heads resemble moose antlers. Their four pairs of eyes resemble tiny slits, which is the reason they have poor vision). Three bambakambo walked on the trail—a mother and two tiny bambakambo that had to be its children. Veronica wasted no time petting the mother (once you get over the initial shock of seeing such a strange creature, it is rather cute). She did not pat the cubs. If she, it was likely that the mother would have spat on her and her chest would have a hole in it, which, of course, would be very inconvenient.

The second interruption was when a tiny icehound, evidently the stupidest of its kind, lunged at her through the shadows. It was a goner before it even lunged. Veronica saw it before it touched her and slashed it repeatedly in midair with tremendous speed, so when it collided with the ground, it split into innumerable ice cubes. The interruption was very brief, but Veronica paused to collect some ice cubes. They were sought after by traders and were valuable.

One hour passed and there were no interruptions. All this time, the forest was becoming more frozen, though it was still afternoon. This was not normal. Mount Vilgroth during the afternoon was usually warm, or, at the very least, mildly cold, unlike its chilling nights.

Veronica was not scared or anxious. Rather, she was overeager. She couldn't wait to get that thing, possibly a robot, for, as any sensible person knows, robots are really cool.

Alas, at the time, Veronica didn't know that she would never reach that prized metal masterpiece that she so longed for. At least, not then.

She was at the edge of the forest now. It was so cold that Veronica was shivering. This was supernatural. Something wasn't right. She looked around, staring through the forest for something out of the ordinary. Nothing. The leaves were a dull green, as usual, topped with snow. Veronica thought the snow was completely natural.

Let's see, thought Veronica. The trees were their usual unsaturated brown with streaks of white. There were no broken twigs. In the distance was a giant tower of black smoke, and there was—

Veronica glanced back at the nine-foot tower of smoke in alarm. It made the dark wood of the trees seem light in comparison. Her eyes were wide. Her thoughts were racing.

"Wha…?" Veronica muttered. Before any further thought came to her, the smoke moved. Well, glided, but it glided exceptionally fast. Veronica gazed in alarm and shock as the smoky *thing* hovered/ran toward her. Before Veronica could run or draw her sword or even blink, the thing was on top of her.

It was a humanoid monster. Its skin looked like hot, dripping ink, swirling and bubbling. It had no hair, and it had empty eye sockets. Instead of a nose was a hole, like that of a skeleton. Its mouth had no lips, nor did it have any teeth except for four fangs, two on the top of the mouth and two on the bottom. The inside of its mouth had no flesh. It was the same dripping ink. The inky skin was dripping from the edge of the mouth. Instead of legs, a black, smoky tail curled in the grass. It was lucky that the bottom part of its body was a tail for it did not have any clothes. It seemed to have no muscles or bones, just that smokey, inky presence. On its back was a column of thick black smoke. And to add to its menacing appearance, the monster had long, smoking fingers ending in extremely sharp tips. "WHAT IN THE—" Veronica exclaimed, but she couldn't finish her sentence.

The horrific monster, who had floated upright, was raising its sharp fingers in a threatening way. Veronica, still lying on the ground, rolled sideways as the monster dug its fingers into the ground where Veronica's head had been just moments before. The grass near the monster's fingers blackened and shriveled into dust within seconds. The monster's mouth widened. The fangs glimmered in the afternoon sun. Veronica grabbed her sword from her bag, jumped up, and slashed at the monster's face.

The blade seemed to pass in slow motion through the monster's head. It was as if she was slashing at water. The monster didn't show the slightest sign of pain, though it seemed a bit more annoyed. The monster's mouth opened wide and let out a terrible, blood-curdling noise.

"SCRRAAAAEEE!!! DIE, PATHETIC HUMAN!"

Veronica jumped out of the way as the monster lunged. The grass underneath its giant, wriggling body was reduced to dust. It turned and floated upright once more. It raised its arms and the monster's hands seemed to be more solid. Veronica felt sick. Black, slimy vines grew out of the monster's palm. The vines inched closer toward Veronica's neck. She slashed at the vines, but her sword phased through them. Veronica walked backward in alarm, out of the reach of the vines. One thought was in her head.

What was this thing?

Without warning, the vines lengthened with extraordinary speed and closed around Veronica's throat. They felt like molten lava. The vines were searingly hot against her skin. As they closed tighter around Veronica's neck, she gasped and sputtered wildly. Her vision was going blurry. All she could see was the vines protruding out of the monster's hand. *What was this thing? What was this thing?* That was all she could think of. All the world was slipping away from her. Veronica's hand unclenched her sword, which fell to the ground with a thump that Veronica could not hear. Everything turned slowly black.

Suddenly, the searing pain stopped. Veronica fell on the dirt next to her sword. Her hearing was becoming clearer.

"Down! Down, you slimy dog! Down, you evil, demonic bihk!" Veronica heard a deep, dry voice cry out.

Her vision was slowly becoming better. First came the ground, then the sky, then the trees. Veronica raised her head to see the oddest sight she had ever seen. The monster was upright, but it was raising its hands to protect itself from the repeated hammering against its slimy skin by what looked like a tree.

No. That couldn't be right. Trees don't have hands.

Veronica squinted at the thing that was hammering the monster. She could see it clearly now. And it was no less peculiar than a tree with hands. In fact, it *was* a tree with hands, though it much more resembled a man. A tall, skinny man. His skin was an uneven coarse wood that stuck out in places. His face looked worn and aged, and his eyes were bright, glowing green. The top of his head had large parts of wood that resembled jagged rocks, jutting out in some spots, making a hollow. He had no nose. Nor did he have a mouth. Instead, the wood stretched over where the nose and mouth would be, making those places relatively flat.

All in all, Veronica had no idea what either of the things in front of her were.

The monster grabbed at the wooden man's wrist as he swung it up to strike once more. It then pulled with all its might, sending the wooden man rocketing to the ground. The wooden man raised his head. He paused, not moving at all. Then he jumped six feet into the air, raised his hand, muttered something under his breath, and a giant green blast of fire shot out of his palm and raced toward the monster, who dissolved into black mist on collision with the fireball.

Veronica was wide-eyed and stunned. Her mouth was half-open in utter shock.

"What in the name of…" Veronica muttered. The wooden man landed on the ground and looked at Veronica. He walked toward her, brushing off the dirt on his arms, and raised his arm out to Veronica, evidently intending to help her up. Veronica did not take his hand. She backed away from the wooden man and got up herself.

"Sorry about that," the tree man said. "That must have been quite… odd."

"WHAT THE—" Veronica started as she staggered away from the wooden man.

"Your leg is injured," interrupted the wooden man. But Veronica continued to limp backward with great speed until her left knee buckled and she toppled to the ground. "I don't suggest walking. But, of course, you are already on the ground."

Veronica got up with difficulty and backed away from the wooden man. "Who in the world are you?"

"My kind dwells not in the mountains," said the wooden man. "Alas, I have forgot to say my name. I am known as Shaman. Just Shaman."

Veronica looked at the wooden man. "Shaman?"

"Yes, Shaman. It is a simple name."

"And may I ask, what are you?" Veronica said, eyeing Shaman suspiciously.

"People ask that," Shaman said simply.

Veronica signaled for him to continue, but he did not. She then asked, "And what was that thing?"

"All in due course," said Shaman, infuriatingly. "Now, if you would please follow me. If you do not want to, that is up to you. I understand it would be hard to trust a tree man you just met. But if you want to stay with that brutally injured leg"—Shaman pointed at Veronica's mangled leg— "have at it."

"I'll take my chances with the leg," Veronica said resolutely. She grabbed a stick and got up, leaning on her stick. She then walked away into the forest. Before she could get too far away from Shaman, he called after her.

"There will be more!" yelled Shaman through the forest. "More of those creatures!" Veronica paused as Shaman appeared through the trees.

"And what exactly are they?"

"Demons," said Shaman. "Monstrous servants of the Magistrate."

Veronica was stunned. "W-what? The Magistrate?"

"Yes!" said Shaman. "The Magistrate."

Veronica stared at Shaman in disbelief. "And why should I believe *you*? You, who came out of nowhere and beat up that over-excited inkblot?"

"Beat up a monster beating up *you*," corrected Shaman truthfully. This made Veronica frown. "I will not stop giving you annoying explanations until you follow me. Then you can get *your* explanations."

Veronica frowned some more, waited for a few seconds, then, at last, said, "Fine…"

Shaman's face lit up. Or rather his eyes, as he had neither a visible nose nor a visible mouth. "Ah, finally. Now, we ought to go. As I say, more omnispectres will come."

"Omniwhat?" stuttered Veronica confusedly.

"The name of the monster that attacked you. Ancient species, but always so hushed up. Enclosed in the land of Nite, mostly. No more waiting, please," Shaman said. He walked over to a nearby tree and to Veronica's confusion, placed his palm on its trunk.

"What are you doing?" asked Veronica. Shaman didn't answer but continued to stare at the trunk.

Then, Shaman muttered, "Quavikh." For a second, nothing happened. Veronica stared at Shaman in mingled confusion. Then, the tree opened as if invisible hands were prying it open. The tree inside was an empty hull with a glowing, swirling, green portal in the middle.

"How!?-" shouted Veronica. Shaman moved out of the way, giving Veronica a clear view of the portal, and gestured for her to go into the portal. Veronica glanced one more time at Shaman and back at the portal. Then, irresolute, she walked through the portal and out of sight.

4

IN THE SAD EXCUSE FOR A REBELLION

VERONICA ENTERED A BEAUTIFUL GRASSY clearing with a variety of plants, flowers, and vines. She looked up at the tree she came out of and saw a tall oak with lush green leaves. There was something majestic about the place and yet something unnatural. She didn't seem to need her stick when she walked in, so she threw it into the forest.

She walked forward into the clearing as Shaman walked through the portal.

"Now, I believe you wanted some explanation?" asked Shaman. Veronica nodded. "Fine. In a word, I am in a rebellion."

"Yes, rebellion," Shaman said in response to the look on Veronica's face.

"Against the Magistrate, I suppose?"

"Yes. Against the Magistrate."

"Then… where are the *rebels?*"

"Ah, yes. There's a lot, really, but… not here. My part of the rebellion is… a work in progress."

Veronica raised her eyebrow. "Yeah, sure."

"I've decided to recruit you," Shaman said. "but not because you're a bounty hunter."

Veronica frowned once more and asked irritably, "Then what *is* the reason? Just spit it out alread—"

"One second," interrupted Shaman. "ECO!" A humanoid person with green, plant-like skin and a head shaped like a plant with a hollow on top emerged. Like Shaman, he had neither a nose nor a mouth, but he did have perfectly circular eyes whose pupils were blue. He was very thin, so thin he looked as if he had not eaten for days, and wearing a dark green tunic.

"This is my apprentice, Eco," said Shaman. "Eco, this is Veronica, a new recruit."

"Hello," said Eco. He and Veronica shook hands briefly.

"Eco, we were just attacked by an omnispectre," Shaman told him. "Please, get some herbs to… cheer Veronica up."

Eco nodded and walked away to the forest.

"Now," Veronica said as she turned to Shaman, "explanations. Now."

"I know, I know. Come with me," said Shaman quickly. The two walked to the side of the clearing and through the trees.

"You see," said Shaman as they walked, "you are a type of person unheard of for years."

Veronica laughed. "Yeah right," she said. "Type of person? What's that supposed to mean?"

"Oh, well…" Shaman said quietly. "Let me show you." He raised his palm and stroked the top of his hand while saying, "Quata." Green light flowed from Shaman's hand like mist. It flew onto the grass, which was turning brown. The green mist flew upon contact with the grass and back into Shaman's palm. The grass was now lush, with fully-grown flowers growing here and there.

"There," said Shaman. Veronica was looking at the grass in awe. She looked at Shaman.

"I never did anything like that. Probably never will."

"But you can do things," Shaman replied. "And you will be able to do what I just did."

"One, that's stupid, and two, how do *you* know I have powers, then?"

"Because of this." Shaman stopped walking, closed his fist, stroked his knuckles, and reopened it with a flourish. A glowing green ball of light flew out of his fingers, which stopped in front of Veronica and started pulsing wildly.

"This is a special type of spell that detects magic in living beings."

"M-magic?" Veronica said. It was not as if she didn't believe Shaman about magic. She had seen him do about three things in one hour that normal people couldn't do even if they tried. But Shaman seemed to be indicating that *she* had powers…

"And what about that monster, hmm? An omnispectre, you called it? Why was it there?"

"To capture you and to take you to the Magistrate, of course."

"And *why*, exactly, would the Magistrate want me?"

"Not just you," corrected Shaman. "Everyone with those *special powers*. Those who have escaped from the Magistrate's clutches at least once, Terren Fallus, for instance, tells us that the Magistrate want to kill them because of their powers. To be specific, their magic powers. We think he's a bit afraid."

Veronica looked at Shaman.

"Yeah, you're nuts," said Veronica. "I'm out."

"Maybe," Shaman replied. "But you do not know where this is, nor do you know how to get back to your mountain."

Veronica blinked a few times. "Okay. Say I do agree to join your rebellion. Say I do have *special powers*. What then? How would you, the plant-guy, and I intend to destroy the Magistrate?"

"Recruiting," stated Shaman. "There are a few magically powerful people out there that haven't been destroyed by the Magistrate."

She looked at Shaman's glowing green eyes. He had proved trustworthy so far... "Last question. Why haven't I seen anyone like you or Eco before in the woods?" Veronica asked.

"We don't come from Mount Vilgroth. I only came because you were there. My species could not survive Mount Vilgroth's cold nights."

Veronica had no more questions. She took a few seconds to think her decision through.

"Fine."

"Hmm?"

"Fine," Veronica said. "I'll join your little rebellion."

"Ah, good!" exclaimed Shaman with energy. "Now this is over, we may go back. I have plans."

"Yes, I suppose."

They walked for a bit until they came upon the light of the clearing, but a horrible sight met their eyes.

"Save y-yourself..." Veronica was standing, looking at Eco, who was dangling in the air, his hands grasping his neck. Squeezing his throat were black, slimy vines coming from a smoking black arm, connected to a smoking black body, with a smoking black head in a wide grin.

"You!" Shaman was running toward Veronica, staring at the monster he called an omnispectre, the same that had attacked Veronica. The omnispectre's mouth widened into a horrific grin, its teeth shiny in the slowly setting sun.

"*You are as good as dead.*" It was a croaky, metallic voice. "*The Magistrate is the most powerful leader this century. He will have your lives.*"

"You'll have to kill me before then!" shouted Shaman, raising his palm and preparing to stroke his wrist.

"*I intend to,*" the omnispectre hissed. Veronica was unsure what to do, though she thought that it was probably better to save Eco. Then again, she barely knew the guy. Or plant? Veronica was still not entirely sure.

The vines squeezed tighter around Eco's neck, slowly growing to wrap around his arms and legs. His head was slowly turning a shade of red, and his pupils were going in every direction. "Save yourself…" he repeated. Eco's voice was higher than ever and his second statement was immediately followed by much choking and sputtering.

"*If you attack, the plant dies,*" croaked the omnispectre. "*Not that it matters,*" it added, smiling its horrible smile. "*No magic in this welp. But I think it won't matter if I bring you in alive or if I bring you in charred, will it?*"

The mouth snapped open without warning. A low hissing came from the beast's throat, as well as an eerie purple light.

Shaman stroked his wrist and yelled, "Bontraka!" A beam of green light flew toward the omnispectre, well-aimed to not hit Eco. Before it could get within a foot radius, raging purple fire hurtled from the omnispectre's throat and out of his mouth as his jaws opened impossibly wide, colliding with the beam of light and extinguishing it instantly.

Shaman ran toward the omnispectre with surprising speed. Veronica thought she may have heard him say something, but Veronica could not hear it over the roar of the flames. A glowing, green, semi-transparent shield formed out of nowhere in front of Shaman. The fire bounced off the shield, not breaking it, but putting large cracks in it. All the time, Veronica was frozen in place.

Shaman tried to reach out for Eco's hand, but with a shout that was louder than the flames, his arm was engulfed in flames. He pulled it back, still groaning. It was charred and smoking, and it looked like Shaman was in extreme pain. The shield was slowly splitting into pieces along its edges, which hovered in midair, in a feeble attempt to still protect Shaman. Veronica guessed that when the shield was completely shattered, they would fall to the ground. The omnispectre grinned, shaking Eco in its hand. Veronica, whose feet were still planted firmly on the dirt, stared, feeling that Shaman would die if she didn't do something. The shield was breaking into large pieces now. It gave a shudder, then, after a few seconds, the shield disintegrated under the pressure of the fire and Shaman ran for his life. Eco was dangling feet away from the flames, looking as if he were about to faint.

The flames were twisting and turning as if it were several writhing snakes. The flames were pointing toward Shaman, growing quickly, cornering him to a dirt wall. The tips of the flames were pointing toward Shaman's heart.

As if it were instinct, Veronica jumped toward the flames and the omnispectre and held her sword in front of her. The flames ricocheted off the metal of the sword and directly into the omnispectre's wide mouth.

"*G-gra-aaah...*" choked the omnispectre. The flames still flowing through the omnispectre's throat, they stopped bursting out of its mouth, as flames were already filling its mouth. He looked like some sort of ugly chipmunk. Soon, all the flames were all in the omnispectre's throat, and, unconsciously, it seemed, it swallowed them. Now, the omnispectre's skin was no longer inky and liquid, but wrinkly and dry, as if it were an oversized raisin.

"*Rraaa!*" the omnispectre roared, dropped Eco, and flew toward Veronica. She pulled out her sword and slashed the monster. The omni-spectre immediately dissolved into mist and floated to the ground, where it disappeared.

"Oof," Veronica told the clearing at large. "Well, that's that."

5

RELLICOS CITY

Shaman lay on a mound of earth and grass, getting his arm doused in a leafy green substance that Eco had concocted. His arm was still charred, black, and wasted, but less so. Parts of the arm were incinerated in the purple fire, which seemed to be more destructive than a normal fire, but the wood was regrowing.

"I am completely fine," Shaman protested. "Get me off this chair now, Eco. I am okay, understand?"

"No," Eco told Shaman without hesitation. Shaman grumbled and looked away from Eco and back to Veronica.

"Where to next?" Veronica asked Shaman.

"Ah, well, assuming you can trust me enough, we will go to Rellicos City to recruit a specific person known to have magical powers."

Veronica believed Shaman about magic and the Magistrate's plans. They explained everything. Everything about the omnispectre that attacked her, everything about Shaman's powers, everything about... well, everything. But Veronica didn't entirely trust Shaman. She reasoned with herself that it was because she barely knew him, but, if she was being honest with herself, it was because Shaman thought she had magical powers, which was, in her mind, impossible. She enjoyed her normal life, and didn't want to be roped into another one.

"No."

"Why not?"

"Because no."

"No?"

"That's what I said. No."

Shaman raised his wooden eyebrows. "You don't trust me." Veronica opened her mouth to speak. No words came out, so she closed it again.

"I'd think that saving your life and you saving mine would be enough, but, alas, it is not. I understand." Veronica frowned.

Shaman sighed. "Ah, there is no point convincing you. I cannot force you. It is your choice. Mount Vilgroth is northwest, one mile away from here." He got up and turned to Eco. "We set out to Rellicos City at once, Eco." His arm was sufficiently healed, which seemed to satisfy Eco. He nodded.

"I bid you adieu," Shaman said to Veronica. Shaman turned and began to walk toward the portal.

"Wait."

Shaman paused and turned back to Veronica. "I'll come," she said. Veronica didn't know exactly why she said it. All she knew was that she had no power, and Shaman did. If another omnispectre came… well, she'd stick with Shaman until she learned a better way to destroy those beasts.

"Thank you. If you are joining us in Rellicos City, you do not need to pack."

Rellicos City. A dark, yet vibrant place, composed of only four types of people: travelers, criminals, noblemen, and police. But mostly travelers and criminals. Its vast expanse stretched miles, skyscrapers piercing the clouds. (Note the past tense.)

This specific part of Rellicos City had one of those skyscrapers with smaller warehouses and buildings in its dark shadow. Not that this darkness mattered. Almost every spot was lit with fancy neon lights coming from every single part of the city, looking very sci-fi. This included from the ground, from the buildings, and from some of the people.

Three indistinct, black-cloaked people pushed through the bustling crowds. "Where to?" inquired Veronica.

"Look for a small, black building," Shaman whispered. "It's a secret base for the Magistrate where Terren is being held."

"How can we look for *any* building with this crowd?" breathed Eco. He looked agitated and was hyperventilating. "I hate this place..."

"Calm down already!" Veronica hissed to Eco. "If you hyperventilate any more, your head will blow up!" Eco grumbled and fell silent.

"There! That's it, I think!" Shaman pointed at a black building. Compared to the skyscrapers, it was a speck of dirt, and no less distinct.

Veronica, Shaman, and Eco half-walked, half-ran toward the building. The building had an obsidian-colored door. Veronica twisted the doorknob and pushed the door open. The room was dark. Very dark. Veronica groped through the darkness for a few seconds before feeling another doorknob. She twisted the doorknob and walked into another room. This one had a lamp on the ceiling, which emitted a faint white light. Her vision was blurred after the impenetrable darkness of the last room. Perhaps that was why the building was divided into a dark area and a light area, to blur intruders' vision. She looked at the other parts of the room. It had what looked like a small wooden table with a chair on one side, but there was nothing else. She did, however, see a lump on the back wall. It was likely that the person who made the wall just got a little careless.

"No one's in here!" called Veronica to Shaman and Eco. They walked to the doorway and looked at the room. When the other walked into the room, they dropped their cloaks onto the floor.

"Hm…" Shaman squinted at the lump on the wall. It seemed that Eco and Shaman also had blurry vision. "I suggest you blink a few times. To take away the blur."

Veronica blinked one or two times. She had clear vision. Now, when she looked closer, she saw that what she thought was a lump on the wall was…

"Terren Fallus." The lump was revealed to be what looked like an extremely realistic statue of Terren Fallus. His mouth was open in a frozen scream, his eyes wide open and staring. His arm was reaching out as if to touch something far away. His body was merged into the flat wall behind it.

"It's a statue of Terren," murmured Veronica. "A really grotesque statue of Terren."

"It isn't a statue." Shaman reached his hand out to touch Terren's forehead. His hand slid down onto his arm, then down to his leg. "It's him. Nearly dead."

"It's *him*?"

"Really evil magic." Eco walked out from behind Shaman. "Really dark. He's trapped inside, and he's frozen in the rock. Must be a powerful dark mage who did it. Only a huge amount of force can…"

"Leave it to me," Veronica told Eco. Veronica pulled back her elbow, clenched her fist, and waited. She aimed for the correct spot, then she punched Terren Fallus straight in his long nose.

"*Aahh…!*"

The stone cracked off Terren's skin, piece by piece. First came his head, then his torso, then his arms and legs. And there he lay on the ground, clutching his nose. A small amount of blood trickled down his left nostril.

"What did you do that for?" He looked up at Veronica, who had a wide grin on her face. "YOU!" he shouted, and he lunged at Veronica. She stepped aside and Terren fell face first into the floor.

"That's enough." Shaman stopped Terren from lunging at Veronica a second time. He turned. "

"Who are you?" he asked.

"My name is Shaman, and, hopefully it was obvious, we're rescuing you." He explained briefly how he met Veronica. Shaman talked quickly and agitatedly. Terren smiled when he was done.

"We haven't met. You operate a different part of the Rebellion?"

"Yes," confirmed Shaman. "Your information about the Magistrate was invaluable. Now, we must go before—"

"Before we come?" said a very deep, raspy, metallic voice.

"Oh, no…" groaned Eco. "No, no, no, no, no…"

Eight omnispectres materialized, forming a semi-circle around Eco, Veronica, Shaman, and Terren. The one who spoke had dark purple ink-skin and was wielding a large black spear. This one looked like the leader. The others wore similar things. One had an axe. Another wore a piece of intricately carved armor, and another had an obsidian helmet. And every single one of them was snarling and baring their teeth.

6

TRADING BLOWS

THE OMNISPECTRES CIRCLED THEM, SNEERING and growling. The one with the spear pointed his weapon at Shaman.

"He knows," rasped the omnispectre with the spear. *"He knows all, yeh f-filthy tree."*

"The Magistrate does not know all," Shaman said to the omnispectre. His chest was out, and his eyes shone with defiance.

"The Magistrate?" the omnispectre laughed a wheezy, croaky laugh. *"Not the Magistrate, no. The Rebellion does not house all the rebels…"* But it did not elaborate on the cryptic statement. Instead, it said, *"You're coming with us."*

"Yes, that seems to be where our problem lies."

"I see no problem."

"I didn't expect you to," said Shaman with a hint of sadness in his voice.

Crack! A second later, Shaman's palm was pressed to the ground, and he was looking at the omnispectres, who were trapped in their own pulsing, slightly transparent green bubbles. They were clawing at them, roaring and yelling horrible and mercifully muffled insults at Shaman.

"Why couldn't you do that with the first omnispectre?" Veronica asked, looking at the bubbles.

"This spell only works with a group. Not very effective with one being. Super inconvenient." He looked around anxiously. "It would be advisable to leave now. They'll get out soon."

They rushed out the doors and through the always moving streets. The crowd was as thick as ever. They were halfway through the street when they heard a terrible noise.

"*Rrraaaaaaa...!*" The spear-wielding omnispectre was bellowing loudly as he searched for Shaman, Veronica, Terren, and Eco. He seemed to be in a horrible temper. The crowd parted significantly. The omnispectre ran at Veronica, like a charging bull.

"Go!" yelled Shaman. They sprinted toward the end of the street and into the huge plaza. Shaman was in the back, shooting fireballs at the omnispectres. They were one-quarter into the plaza when Shaman hit one. The omnispectre flew back and hit yet another omnispectre. Both creatures ricocheted off each other and bounced in different directions. Something caught Terren's eye.

"My sword!" Veronica turned around just in time to see Terren running directly toward a sword that the still bouncing omnispectre dropped on collision with the other omnispectre. *That idiot,* Veronica thought. Now that she looked at it, she saw that it was, as she expected, Terren's golden sword. Just as Terren grasped it, one of the running omnispectres grabbed his back and wrenched him up, opening its jaw, looking as if it planned to have dinner with Terren's head.

It was sheer luck that the bouncing omnispectre stopped bouncing and ran back to Terren at that moment. Just as the omnispectre in front of him opened its mouth to eat, it was pushed out of the way by the other omnispectre, who was dry and raisin-like because of Shaman's fireball. He promptly dropped Terren and stumbled toward Veronica in a rage. Veronica, on instinct, slashed at the omnispectre's face. The head dissolved before the body, and the body fell to the ground and turned to smoke. The omnispectre that was pushed aside let out a burst of purple flame, aimed at her. Veronica held up her sword and the fire ricocheted back onto the spear-wielding omnispectre's arm. It let out a shriek and fell to the ground, grasping its arm. The omnispectre vomiting flame at Veronica was still doing so. Veronica twisted her sword slightly, sending it into the omnispectre's chest. Disconcerted, the monster stopped shooting flames from its mouth. Veronica sank her sword into the omnispectre's chest, sending it reeling and slowly evaporating into smoke.

"You're welcome," Veronica said to Terren.

"Th-thanks," stuttered Terren, then he shivered and gave a quiet whimper. He looked pathetic. He got up, and they realized that they were very behind in the fight. Shaman and Eco had paused for Veronica and Terren, and, consequently, they ended up battling two omnispectres each. Veronica quickly tracked all omnispectres on her fingers. Two dead, one injured, one bouncing away through the crowd, and four battling Shaman and Eco.

"Shrabakh!" shouted Terren, holding up his sword and stroking the middle of it. The sword split in two, like a raven's beak, and from the inside of the sword came a ball of yellow fire that split into four in midair and hit an omnispectre each. They were like tracking missiles. The omnispectres staggered and writhed as the fireballs sank into their skin. All Veronica had to do was swipe her sword, and they turned into smoke. The burnt omnispectre got up, still staggering slightly, and jumped at Shaman. A slash, and Veronica had cut off the omnispectre's arm.

"*Aaaaahhh aa-aaaaahhh!*" the monster let out. It dropped in midair, letting out volleys of flame out of pain. It writhed and wriggled on the floor, like an ugly wrinkled worm.

The two other omnispectres were backing away from Veronica, obviously afraid. She started forward threateningly, and they ran, squealing into the distance.

Then the bouncing omnispectre, who had seemingly attained better weaponry and armor when it flew directly through a shop window, sprinted toward Shaman, raising a massive hammer, and wearing strong black armor.

Terren flew in front of Shaman just as the omnispectre raised its hammer. The hammer came crashing down toward Shaman's head… and it was stopped. The omnispectre gave a confused grunt. Terren had blasted the side of the hammer that was going to smash into Shaman with a light shockwave from his sword, not enough to destroy it, but enough to stop it in midair. Remember now, that this omnispectre was already hit with a fireball, making it solid. So, when Terren grabbed the hammer out of the confused omnispectre's hands, lifted it into the air, and smashed it on the omnispectre's skull, everything went according to plan. Not for the omnispectre, though.

When Terren cleared the smoke from his vicinity, he walked back to the group. "I like you guys," he declared. Terren looked at Veronica and frowned. "Most of you guys," he added. His frown deepened. *Ungrateful bihk,* Veronica thought. *I saved your life around three times in the last three minutes.*

"That's all good, but we still have one more problem," said Shaman, pointing at the remaining omnispectre.

"Oh, let it survive," Veronica said. "The Magistrate is going to kill him anywa-"

BLAM!

A flash of purple light shot out of nowhere. It hit the omnispectre in the back, disintegrating it immediately. Another flash of light. The second beam hit Veronica in the chest, sending her flying backwards.

7

THE DARK MAGE

VERONICA LANDED ON THE HARD asphalt, but there was no serious damage. Shaman ran over urgently. "Up, up! Get up!"

Veronica quickly got up and asked, *"What was that?"* She was shoved forward by Shaman, who was staring unblinkingly at something in the far distance. His hands were trembling, and he was shaking his head, as if in disbelief.

"GO! NOW!" he yelled at Veronica, Terren, and Eco. Terren was also staring at the same thing in the distance.

"I agree with this guy," he said, pointing at Shaman, who looked a little offended that he had been called "this guy." He overlooked it and pushed them away. He ran a bit forward and muttered something Veronica could not hear.

After he muttered, Shaman raised his hand and did a flicking motion with his index and middle fingers, as if shooing off an annoying fly. A portal opened, just like the one that opened in the tree. "Get inside! Get inside, now! A Rebellion member is on the other side to meet you!

Go!" He shunted Eco in first, then Veronica. Then, Shaman tried to shove in Terren, but just as he lifted his foot to go inside, a blast of purple light hit him between the shoulder blades. It expanded quickly until it was as if he were in a glowing purple bubble that enveloped his entire body. He was frozen inside.

The dot in the distance got closer and closer, and it got more and more distinguishable as a person. An extremely thin person. Veronica could see it's ribs through its cloak, which was black and purple. Its hands were black-gloved. The cloak fell past its feet, and it dragged behind the figure. Its hood completely shadowed its face. In its hand was glowing purple fire, flickering, and twisting, as if it were alive.

Before Veronica could comprehend what she was seeing, the thing stopped walking. It raised its other arm, and as if pulling on an invisible rope, made the bubble that Terren was trapped in move toward it.

"Vokhi," the thing muttered quietly in a high, sharp voice. This was obviously some sort of spell like the ones that Shaman used, as the fire in its hand flew out like ropes from its palm and pierced Terren's bubble. The bubble, as bubbles would do, popped. The flaming ropes wrapped themselves around Terren's body and flew through his mouth into his body. He seemed to be in unimaginable pain, though he was clearly still alive. Veronica and Shaman stood frozen in horror at the gruesome sight.

The fire stopped flowing out of the thing's hand. The last bits of flame shot into Terren's mouth, and he lay on the ground, breathing heavily and uneasily. Shaman stepped forward, just when he thought that all was fine. But all was not fine. Veronica watched, stiff as a board, as Terren's skin suddenly turned to fire.

"Aaaaahhh… *Aaaaahhh!*" screamed Terren, sounding remarkably like a very small child throwing a temper tantrum. Veronica would have laughed if it wasn't so horrific. His form was still human, but the fire seemed to envelop him like lava, flowing onto him, leaving him in seemingly endless, excruciating pain.

"I have Terren," the mage said. "All I need is you, Shaman. Both of you are needed by the Magistrate." Seemingly not hearing the mage, Shaman jumped on what Veronica thought must have been some sort of dread demon. He raised his fist, preparing for a fireball. Before he could blast his foe, however, the mage grabbed Shaman's hand with his gloved one and pushed it back. Shaman's other hand clasped the man's arm and pinned it to the ground. With his free hand, the mage thrust his hand in front of Shaman's face and yelled, "Slaksatirakh!" Shaman flew back immediately and hit the ground hard, drifting into unconscious.

The mage flicked his arm, and Terren's skin went back to normal, though he was still twitching horribly, and his eyes were closed. He turned his back to the concrete of the Rellicos City Border and pleaded to thin air, "H-help me..."

Veronica glanced at Terren, twitching on the ground, then at Eco, whimpering in fear, and at the man, who was staring at her from behind its shadowy hood. She rolled her eyes, and, bringing out her sword, ran toward the thing looking at her. The sword slashed at the mage, but he dodged the blade and grabbed its hilt. He pulled, and Veronica was sent flying into the concrete.

"Veronica Korix, you are *irrelevant* to this matter, so *get out of it!*" he screeched, taking out a small, shiny, two-sided spike with intricate engravings in it. The mage threw it at Veronica's face, but Veronica jumped out of the way. The spike flew past her. Veronica glanced back at it. It was still airborne, and it seemed to be turning slowly in Veronica's direction! As it did so, it split into two perfect, equally sharp and deadly halves. Veronica ducked as a second wave of spikes flew at her from behind. They shot into the mage's gloved hand, and he caught them.

"Yeah, I think I'm good," she said, thinking quickly of a strategy. The mage took a step forward.

"Well, then..." he told her "...this is not going to end well for you..." Veronica was thinking fast. Finally, she settled on a wild, outrageous idea.

It could backfire at any moment if she attempted it. But it was the only option. What other choice did she have?

"Uh… um… hey, what's that big thing in the distance over there?" she said loudly, pointing over the mage's shoulder.

Veronica's plan had worked. The mage turned his head to look over its shoulder, which gave Veronica enough time to grab both Terren and Shaman and sprint for the portal. Eco, who watched the whole battle, was shaking madly, but followed swiftly. Before she could take another step, Veronica felt a tug, and realized that the mage was holding on to Shaman's limp leg. He had a very strong grip for such a thin and weak-looking man. Veronica tugged and tugged, but the man wouldn't let go.

"*Veronica Korix…*" he said in a dangerous voice. "*You have made a grave mistake on this day! I swear on the Lands of the Dead that-* "

"Oh, *shut up,* won't you!" Veronica yelled as she kicked him in the forehead. The force knocked Veronica back. She let go of Shaman and flew face first into snow. The portal behind her had closed. Eco pulled Veronica up and she spat snow out of her mouth. She looked at him. His face was very pale.

"Are you all right?" she asked. Eco pointed to something behind Veronica. She turned. There lied Terren splayed on the snowy ground. Veronica turned to see Shaman. He wasn't there.

"You left him behind," said Eco dully. "You let go. I don't blame you. However, that dark mage has him, now."

"Excuse me, what?" said Veronica, making a confused face. "Dark mage?"

"Well, it's an ancient term," said Eco, shrugging, "For someone who has magical powers that uses their powers for good or bad. A dark mage is bad. Very, very bad. Shaman told me."

"Well, I'm very sorry about Shaman. That… thing is ruthless," she apologized. "I'm also really sorry about… him."

Veronica nudged Terren's head with her foot. He jerked and said, in an annoyed voice, "hZ was that for!?" He got up and frowned. "I don't know about you, but we seem very *lost*."

Veronica scanned their surroundings. They were. It was a vast plane of ice and snow. The tips of the rocky mountains in the very far distance were hidden by clouds.

"An ant could recognize as much," Veronica said, annoyed. She looked at the sky. The sun was setting.

At this point, Terren stumbled back down onto the snow. His leg was broken. "Let's find shelter," she said, looking at Terren. "We'll need it if this *idiot is* hurt. In the morning, we search for that Rebellion member. Then we can try finding Shaman. Eco, you're obviously knowledgeable on magic. You can tell me about it."

Veronica had been away from her home on Mount Vilgroth for an entire day. Not that this bothered her. She had been gone from home much longer than this on other occasions, but it always made her feel a bit uneasy. They were sleeping in a sort of igloo-tent they had made. Eco made most of it, but a large piece of ice fell on his head, so Veronica had to finish it. As they did not have sleeping bags, Terren proposed that they move the snow in a way that they acted as pillows for sleep. But someone had to do the night watch.

"I think I should do it," Terren said, standing upright. Eco had found a long, thin icicle from a nearby cave that Terren had used for a walking stick. He had to wait for his leg to heal.

"I don't see why I can't," said Eco. He was still rubbing his plant-shaped head.

"Eco, I think you have a really bad head injury," said Veronica. "If something like that dark mage or whatever you call it comes…" Eco twitched, obviously uncomfortable at the thought of an evil sorcerer sneaking up on him in the dead of night. "And forgive me for saying so, but I don't really think it's best to put my life *and* Eco's into your inept hands." said Veronica, looking at Terren disdainfully.

"Both of you have injuries," Veronica continued. "I'll do it, as I'm not hurt, and I probably won't die in the first five seconds of danger."

So, there she stood, looking out onto the extensive snowfields. She could see absolutely nothing. The only thing active was the wind blowing the snow into different formations. Not a sign of life except from inside their ice cabin. And she would have to do *this* for three hours. Veronica half-hoped that some demon or dragon would attempt to blow down the cabin.

Her mind wandered from thought to thought, such as what she could be doing if she didn't volunteer to be on night watch, and what would have happened if something bad happened to Terren on his turn. She smiled at that thought.

Veronica's thoughts wandered to the dark mage. *Who was he? What is even a 'he?' Was the 'he' a 'she' or an 'it?'*

Veronica wondered and wondered until her shift was done.

8

WAYLOC

VERONICA WENT TO SLEEP AT 1:00 in the morning. She was sleeping on a mat of snow, shaped at the top, as Terren had proposed, to form makeshift pillows. Her gear was beside her. Speaking of Terren, he did not exactly snore but instead breathed so loudly that Veronica could have sworn that the cabin was rumbling.

Eco was outside, fully healed, looking, as Veronica had done, over the dark snowy grounds. Veronica was still awake, listening for any hint of danger, or anything, really, other than the howling winds outside to take her mind off her immense boredom. *If only,* Veronica thought. A few minutes later, she drifted to sleep

Veronica was awoken by a yell. A yell she recognized as Eco's. She flew upward, grabbed her sword and gun, and ran outside, pausing only to kick Terren in his mostly healed leg, waking him up.

"What is it, Eco?" Veronica inquired. Eco looked startled and panicked. Terren ran to Eco's side, and he followed his gaze. His eyes widened.

"L-look," Terren told Veronica. He pointed to something in the distance. Veronica squinted at it. That "it" was a man. The man was almost impossible to see, as he wore a long, white cloak. But the edges of the cloak, which were lined with gold silk, stood out most clearly from the snowy background. He was carrying a long, wooden staff, and his cloak covered his face. It did not, however, cover his beard, which was at least a foot long.

They all waited for the man to get closer. And closer he came. A few tense minutes later, they were less than twenty feet away from each other. On closer inspection, Veronica saw that the man was very thin, but not as thin as the dark mage they saw. The top of the staff he held wrapped around a shiny, white jewel. His pale, wrinkled hands were clenched around it.

He cleared his throat, obviously feeling uncomfortable from the awkward silence. "You are part of the Rebellion?" His voice was clear but slightly dry. Whoever he was, he was obviously very old. *As if his beard wasn't an obvious clue.*

"Yes," Eco said. "You're a mage, right?" "Indeed," said the man. He unhooded himself to reveal a bald head, long nose, and sharp gray eyes. He was even more wrinkly than Lian. He was ancient. "I am Wayloc. You are Shaman's pupils, I believe. You shall come with me."

"And why is that?" Veronica said loudly. She stared suspiciously at Wayloc.

Wayloc smiled. "Shaman had more than your little group and himself in the Rebellion."

"Um, we know," Eco said.

Wayloc's smiled lessened. "Oh, well, that's convenient. I was going to make a joke about fan clubs, lighten the atmosphere, you know, but now it'd just be weird. The point is, I'm in the Rebellion."

"Well, that all seems in order," said Terren. He walked over to Wayloc's side.

"Wait," said Eco. "We don't know for sure if he's trustworthy. I'll ask him a ques—"

"Shaman is a thikhbog, a tree-dwelling human sub-species. His flesh color is usually green. He is a mage, and you are his apprentice. He speaks of you often," said Wayloc in a rush.

Eco looked surprised, and he walked right beside Wayloc, shaking his hand. "Veronica, you're coming, right?"

Veronica stared into Wayloc's eyes. "Hm… well, I suppose." Like with Shaman, she didn't trust him too much. Nevertheless, she walked toward Shaman's other side, right beside Eco.

"Come with me, if you will," Wayloc told the three. "I have an acceptable cave."

Veronica felt a strong urge to smile. Any cave in existence would be less wet than their old ice cabin, which still stood behind them. As they walked, a fog grew behind them, consuming the igloo.

"I am, in fact, close friends with Shaman," said Wayloc. "And I have been for a very long time."

"That's nice," said Eco. "He mentions me?"

"Yes, he seems quite fond of you, especially. Shaman had made sure that I was at least two miles from the rendezvous point, in which you were supposed to stand."

"'You?' What does 'you' mean?" Veronica asked.

"You, Eco Camellan, and Terren Fallus."

"What about Shaman?"

"Well, when he told me, I got the feeling that he didn't expect himself to come. And sadly, the Rebellion can't afford to search for him just yet."

Veronica pondered that thought on the grueling walk to the mountains, Wayloc talking all the way. The group quickly discovered that

Wayloc was like Shaman in demeanor, but unlike Shaman in several ways. For one thing, he was very strict, and not as caring as Shaman was.

"You're all as slow as turtles! Quickly! I'm supposed to train you," he urged.

"Train us in… what?" Veronica inquired curiously. She put her mind off Wayloc's words.

"Shaman tells me that you cannot channel magic yet, and Terren can only channel it through objects." Wayloc looked at Terren's sword, which he had brought from the ice cabin. Terren looked insulted. Veronica shrugged. She was not bothered by Wayloc's words, except for the word "yet."

After about a mile of walking, they came across the massive mountains. A cave entrance was inside an especially large mountain. It did not look naturally formed, as if someone had carved it with their bare hands.

"Ah," said Wayloc, looking at the cave. "Rendezvous point sweet rendezvous point."

Terren looked inside the dark, dank cave. "Not very fit for human habitation," he noted.

"Ah, I'll see to that," Wayloc murmured. He pointed his staff to a space on the ground, and exclaimed, "Trobrin!" Instantly, what looked like liquid wood poured out from his staff, which solidified into a smooth lump on contact with the ground.

"Now for the fire," Wayloc muttered again. "Yes, especially important. Vox!" A small fireball shot out of Wayloc's staff and collided with the wood, setting it on fire.

"Go on. Warm up now," he told the three people behind him. "I'll create some better living conditions."

Veronica, who was, at this point, unsurprised by this feat of magical prowess, sat around the fire in one of the stubby little stools that Wayloc had conjured up. Terren and Eco had already sat down. "Get a good rest, you'll wake up early tomorrow," Wayloc said to them. He was in the middle of making a cabinet.

"Why would we need a cabinet?" Terren asked.

"Decoration!" Wayloc exclaimed. "We are not barbarians."

Terren shrugged and turned back to the fire. Like the others, his hands were put in front of the flickering flames. And like everyone else, he was smiling from the warmth. This was better than anything they had experienced on their journey so far.

9

THE DEMON DOG AND THE CORRUPTED CAT

"Veronica Korix! Training will have to pause."

Thank the gods, Veronica thought. Wayloc had explained that they had to train so they could hone their skills, as they would need them to help fight the Magistrate. The training was both dull and difficult. First, it was dull. Veronica had to stare at a wooden ball Wayloc had created, repeating the spell "tlik" repeatedly. Wayloc had demonstrated the spell, which was supposed to nudge objects.

"Tlik. Tlik. *Tlik*," Veronica repeated, mentally urging it to move with all her brainpower. And absolutely nothing happened.

Wayloc sighed. "No, no, it's *tlik*. With a shorter *ik*. Rhymes with 'click.'" Veronica got extremely annoyed.

Then came the difficulty. Wayloc felt that looking at a ball for two hours was a waste of valuable time. Instead, she was supposed to run six miles across the snowfields with ten-pound weights on her back, repeating the spell 'vox' the whole time. As if that wasn't a waste of time. Obviously, the work was hard.

So, here she was. Wayloc had paused training, and she was feeling extremely grateful. "Is there any sort of issue?" she asked. "Other than, of course, your unnatural strictness with training," she added, hoping Wayloc would take a hint.

"I may be strict, but I am fair," Wayloc said, looking regal in his white and gold cloak.

"I don't see Terren having such a hard time. I don't see Eco having a hard time either." Terren was staring at a wall, eyes wide, back hunched, and he wasn't blinking. Eco was practicing sword fighting, as he could not practice magic, with a human-sized, wooden dummy.

"Oh, trust me when I say I am giving Mr. Fallus as much pain as I am giving you." Wayloc then proceeded to whack Terren's arms and legs, shouting, "Straight and tall, now!"

"What about Eco?" Veronica asked rather accusingly.

"Why don't you see for yourself?" He tapped the dummy on which Eco was practicing with his staff. As quick as a bullet, it sprung to life, ripped off its arm, and used it like a whip against Eco. Eco swiped his weapon, a flimsy wooden sword, in the air this way and that with ease.

"I'm not insulting your magic, but this is pretty easy!" Eco shouted over the thumping of wood against wood.

Wayloc smiled coldly and said, "Suit yourself." He held the dummy's head in place and murmured, "Polmorgiin." The head started to morph, and so did the rest of the body. It seemed to melt into an invisible mold. A few seconds later, a wooden jaguar-sized wolf stood where the dummy had, dodging Eco's attacks.

"Really?" Eco said, half-laughing. "This is easier than before!"

"Wait for it," Wayloc told him, his smile wide. The wolf opened its wooden jaws, and a burst of fire shot out of its mouth. The fire ignited Eco's white shirt. He let out a yell and patted the fire out with his hand.

"Now," Wayloc said, turning to Veronica. "I must know why you battled the dark mage a few days ago."

"Why?"

"Well, apart from the mage being one of the last and most dangerous in the world, you have attracted the attention of the Magistrate."

"How do you know? And how did I get his attention?"

"That mage is his most feared and most powerful warrior, his greatest general, and his very best assassin. You attacked him. Word has spread throughout the Rebellion."

"I attacked him?!" Veronica said loudly. "If anything, he attacked me!"

"I know, I know," Wayloc said quickly. "But the point is, the Magistrate's efforts are now more focused on you and Terren. And let me tell you, if I'm not mistaken, he'll probably rip you to shreds with his axe then toss your remains into a fire, or something like that. Or worse."

"Very specific. Is that all?" Veronica asked, not eager to get back to training.

"Yes, I suppose it is." Wayloc turned to Terren and frowned. "I don't like him," Wayloc said to no one in particular. "He tries to have a strong personality, but it's mostly an act." He walked away.

Yay, me. Back to training. Veronica was heading back toward the exit to the cave when Wayloc called back to her. "Wait!" Wayloc walked toward her once more. "I've taken a liking to you. You can do the easy things, like weightlifting fifteen-pound rocks."

Veronica longed to say, "Wow, so easy." But she thought better of it. So, she got a large rock from the side of the cave, sat on a staff-made chair, and lifted it into the air, then down again, then up, then down again, to be repeated for some time.

"How does this *magic* work anyways?" Veronica asked. Wayloc turned and smiled.

"Good question," he asked. He brought out his staff, made a second magic chair, and sat on it. "Cease your weight-lifting for now." Veronica dropped the rock on the side of her chair.

"Magic is created in people randomly," the mage said. "It is not hereditary. On these very rare occasions, magic forms in living things right around"—Wayloc pointed to a part just above his heart— "here. It's theorized that magic is a shapeless thing, like water. It contains all the true elements."

"Do you mean the periodic table?"

Wayloc frowned. "*The periodic table...* nonsense. All the elements there exist, but I'm talking about the *magical* elements, the old elements, like fire, earth, water, etc. It's been added on, of course. The current elements are 'Fire, Water, Earth, Chaos, Shadows, and Light.'"

"Hm," Veronica said. "Thanks. But how can it do stuff like create fireballs, or make things fly? It doesn't make sense. It defies physics. And did magic have anything to do with the Remaking? And the dark mage mentioned a 'Land of the Dead?'"

Wayloc went a bit pale. "No one can say for sure how magic creates spells. We will likely never know *how* the Remaking occurred. And only two people alive today know about the Land of the Dead, and they likely will never reveal the sacred information."

"But... "

"Okay, you got your explanation," Wayloc interrupted. "I need to send a message to my friends at the Rebellion, Molis and Krifnot. They should know when we can storm the Magistrate's fortress. Now back to work."

It was one hour later when it happened. A violent burst of hot wind suddenly enveloped the cave. Veronica opened her mouth to say something, then closed it. All of them were startled,

Veronica swore, and so did Terren, but no one heard them, not even themselves, for a violent, tumultuous, ringing explosion erupted directly outside the cave just as Veronica began saying something in response to the odd burst of wind. Dust, rocks, and pebbles started to fly everywhere, namely in Veronica, Eco, and Terren's direction. Veronica dropped the rock she was holding in shock as an opaque cloud of debris hid Eco and Terren's startled faces from view.

She coughed from inhaling dust. She tried to wave the dust away so she could see what happened to everyone else, but to no avail. Her ears were still ringing from the thunderous explosion.

Wayloc's voice rang out through the mist. "Rilbrokh!" The dust subsided suddenly, and Veronica could see Wayloc, his hand raised, Terren, his eyes wide, and Eco, breathing heavily.

"What the klobtra was that!?" Veronica shouted.

"Him," Wayloc said, looking past the demolished cave and what once was an entrance. Around thirty or forty feet away from the cave entrance was the dark mage, still draped in a black and purple cloak.

"Oh, Wayloc, how I've longed to see you," the mage said, his voice full of evil and menace, topped with a whole lot of sarcasm. "I'd love to chat sometime," he said. "But I'm not here for you. I'm here for Terren Fallus and, most especially, Veronica Korix. And believe me, Wayloc, I will collect them."

"Over my dead body."

The mage made a motion with his head to show he was rolling his eyes under his hood. "Ever the valiant hero. But do not worry, your death will happen soon enough." The mage chuckled. "Look at us here, talking. I've been wasting my own time."

The evil mage pulled out the long, two-sided spike he had attacked Veronica with. He broke it into two perfect halves and placed each one on his different side. He flicked his index finger on his right hand backward. A cloud of purple mist briefly appeared, hiding everything from view, and then there were two creatures. One, a large, orange, black, and red jaguar with huge bat-like wings the size of a lion, and another, a big, glittering dog made completely of ice and crystals with long, sharp teeth. Both animals were unconscious.

"My demon dogs died long ago," the mage continued, in response to the confused looks on everyone else's faces. "Their souls still lie in these… well, spike-weapon-heat-seeking things. Whatever you call them. Haven't come up with a good name yet. But now, I have obtained two hosts for them to bond with: a jaguan"—a shapeshifter, to those who do not know—"and an icehound I found nearly dead in the darkest depths of Mount Vilgroth. It seemed that it was recovering from an attack with a person who must have had the exceptional skills of, dare I say, a bounty hunter?" His head twitched toward Veronica.

He turned back to Wayloc. "But the Magistrate, most highly of demonic warlords, thinks that his needs far outweigh mine, to focus on capturing more of the magically gifted, and to leave alone the trivial matters of necromancy."

"Leave this place, Mendellan, and I will spare you," said Wayloc.

"*Don't call me that!*" the mage shouted. He raised his hand and shouted to the afternoon, "Nixrava!" Cords of black smoke bound Wayloc where he stood.

The others took that as their cue to fight. Everyone started in almost perfect unison toward the mage. The mage moved his hands together, and a large, purple, glowing, transparent bubble surrounded him and expanded toward the group. Encased in his bubble, the mage said, seemingly to himself:

"Morgrim, Spectre, I bring you back from the land of no return to serve your master, die for your master, kill for your master!" the mage said dramatically deep, rumbling voice. Meanwhile, the bubble, which had expanded so that Veronica had a foot of moving distance, was still slowly growing to the edges of the cave. Out of the corner of her eye, she saw Terren try to punch the bubble. She could hear his slight moan of pain. Apparently, the mage heard this, as well.

"Oh, don't worry," the mage said in response to Terren's momentary pain. "Do you really think I'd bring you to the Magistrate crushed? How am I supposed to hold you when you're crushed?"

The two spikes next to the mage were shuddering violently and erupting into opaque black smoke. Veronica, as well as the others, were exactly one centimeter away from the pulsing bubble. Eco, she saw, was putting his hand, with difficulty, on the pulsing bubble. He tapped it, also with difficulty, and seemed to be urging his finger to do something. The spikes were rattling so violently that they briefly jumped around left and right.

Suddenly, a green spike sprung out of the middle of Eco's finger. (This caused him a great deal of pain, as his eyes were watering.) This punctured the bubble at last. As it evaporated, rather than popped, Veronica was the first to run toward the mage. He turned his head toward her as she drew out her sword, jumped up, and prepared to kick him in midair, but something hard collided with her as she was a few centimeters away from the mage.

Veronica flew sideways and landed relatively smoothly on the stone ground. The thing that collided with her was a massive dog, the one that, she knew, was the icehound that she had battled two days before. But the crystals it was covered in were tinted purple, and it seemed to radiate a sinister darkness. It now was covered in spikes of crystal. Its claws and teeth were made of bone and were twice as sharp. Its head was wider and more distorted, and its eyes glowed purple. Behind the dog was a cat, whose face was just as wide, with spiky black and purple hair and glowing purple eyes, thin and slanting. It had long, bony wings that would have been more suited with a bat. It was thinner than the dog.

"Say hello to Morgrim and Spectre," the mage introduced. "They were my pets long ago, and they succumbed to death. I have revived them." The mage chuckled. "A pity no ones going to revive you."

Eco jumped forward and tackled the mage. "What the…" the mage exclaimed as Eco's fist sank into his chest. Eco exclaimed and fell back, gripping his fist. Startled into action, the two beasts sprung forward toward Veronica.

The winged cat, Spectre, zoomed through the air, its wings flapping, growling alarmingly at Veronica. The dog was running. Terren flew out of nowhere to tackle Morgrim, and Veronica slid to the side as the jaguar flew past. Spectre turned and landed with a small *thunk* on the stone. It opened its wide jaws and flaming spikes flew out of the deep depths of its throat.

"Oh, of course, you can do that!" Veronica yelled sarcastically, trying hard to avoid the spikes. Suddenly, she was dragged by glowing purple ropes to the ground. The mage had cast a spell on all of them. He breathed heavily as he watched his handiwork. They were all bound by the same purple ropes that held Veronica.

"You may wonder," the mage said, "how I have found you." Veronica could tell, under the hood, the mage was grinning. "I put a tracker on Terren Fallus, while he was under the unendurable pain the vokhi curse causes."

Eco gritted his teeth (behind, of course, the strip of skin that covered his mouth). "Who are you?"

The mage turned, but it was not he who responded. Wayloc's voice rang through the ruins of the cave. "His name is Mendellan, otherwise known as Mendelo, darkest of all mages, embodiment of malice."

10

MASTER OF MALICE

THE MAGE, APPARENTLY NAMED MENDELO, looked at Wayloc, bound by black-smoking ropes, and Veronica knew that he was no longer smiling. However, his voice was the same tone.

"Yes, thank you for saying the obvious," Mendelo said. "My name *is* Mendelo, soon-to-be killer of"—he glanced at all of them— "all of you, really."

Terren chuckled. Mendelo turned on him. "Something funny?"

"Well, yes," Terren said. "I mean, Wayloc said your name so *dramatically,* but it didn't have much of an impact, did it? It's just a strange name, that's all!"

The mage continued to look at Terren. "I'm going to assume you just said that involuntarily, because that is an exceptionally stupid thing to tell a dark mage." He raised his hand and pointed it toward Eco's face. "Maybe this will convince you to be a bit more respectful in your last hours before the Magistrate kills you."

Mendelo looked at "Sorry, I don't need a new houseplant, thanks." Mendelo chuckled. "I think your friend Shaman will take that role."

Eco's eyes widened. Mendelo's palm was glowing bright purple. Veronica knew that if she didn't act fast, Eco would be a pile of vines. She bent down. Her sword was in her scabbard. As her hands were tied, she could not do anything but grab the sword with her teeth, which would be completely uncivilized. Morgrim and Spectre were at Mendelo's side once more, and their eyes were fixed on Eco's face, which looked horrified.

Veronica's free index finger nudged a gap in the ropes and pulled them apart, freeing one of her hands. She did the same with her other index finger. She pulled her sword out of the scabbard and ran silently toward Mendelo, whose head was turned and whose palm was glowing so brightly that it made the sun outside dim in comparison. The mage's head turned toward the source of footsteps, but it was too late. Veronica swung the sword at Mendelo's neck, but the sword vibrated in places on collision as Mendelo keeled back, gripping his neck. "Kill her! Kill her!"

Morgrim jumped forward and swiped his claws at her face, a blow that she dodged. Luckily so, for as the claws swung through the air, a trail of fire followed each sharp end. In midair, Veronica hit the giant dog with the flat end of her blade, sending him flying back. Spectre vomited a wave of flaming spikes at her once again, and Veronica dodged.

What is with evil bihks and fire? Veronica thought as a second volley of flaming spikes hurled their way toward her head. This time, she dodged all of them except one, which scraped her shoulder.

Veronica threw her sword at Spectre, sending the cat crashing to the ground in pain as the sword collided. She picked up her sword and threw it in the other direction. Mendelo laughed.

"Were you even trying to hit me?! Because you failed."

Veronica smiled darkly. "No, I wasn't."

Mendelo looked at where the sword had hit. It had destroyed the ropes that bound Wayloc. He was standing, holding his staff, which was pointed toward Mendelo. "Time to leave."

Mendelo backed away, straightening his cloak, and making sure his face was still in shadow. "Wayloc, we both know you don't have the ability to kill me. So, we'll just have to battle over and over because you'll never find the tracker on Terren Fa—oh, you found the tracker on Terren Fallus."

Wayloc had pointed his staff at Terren and drew from his chest a small pulsing purple orb. He raised his eyebrow. "Well, this is not the end, even if you have found my... my..." Wayloc's staff point suddenly had a long, sharp, very fatal-looking edge made of pulsing white light, making the staff into a spear.

"I suggest you leave."

Mendelo ran, and he disappeared in a swirl of purple smoke just as Wayloc threw the staff-spear at the place where Mendelo's head was just a millisecond before. After he disappeared, he raised his palm, and his staff flew into it.

"Well, pack up. We're moving," he announced.

"Uh..." Eco said, but Terren finished his sentence for him.

"We're still stuck."

"Ah, yes," Wayloc said awkwardly, as he prepared to sever their bonds.

The next day was Moving Day. Veronica was awakened by Wayloc's quiet calls to her. She was glad to be awake. Her disturbing dreams were full of hooded figures repeatedly chanting, "You cannot escape," an unsettling sight for anyone sensible.

Veronica got up. "What?" she called back.

"We need to talk."

A few minutes later, Wayloc and Veronica were walking along a long strip of cave next to the first.

"Mendelo was once known as Mendellan Kroth," he told her. She nodded. "He lived long ago. And he should be dead."

"W-what?" This news was quite unexpected.

"Yes. Mendelo should be dead. Very, very, very dead."

"How come?"

"Well, if you want it simply, he's one thousand twenty-four years old." Veronica's eyes widened slightly. "And he was blasted head first into a jagged rock." She blinked one or two times. "While falling into a volcano."

"He seems pretty dead to me."

"Yes, except…"

"That he's somehow still alive, yeah," Veronica finished. "I got that already."

"We've—that is to say, the Rebellion—has no idea what the Magistrate himself is capable of. For all we know, he could be capable of necromancy. Bringing the dead back to life," Wayloc added, in response to Veronica's slightly bewildered look. "Dark business. Really old. And near impossible."

"How do you know how he died?"

"Well, if you want the truth, I'm also around one thousand twenty-four years old," Wayloc admitted. "I witnessed his alleged death. But I don't think that's the point."

Veronica blinked a few times. "And why would you be telling me this?"

"Pack up the bags," Wayloc said quickly. "The others should be stirring by now."

After the battle in the cave, Veronica wasn't too surprised that Eco kept thanking her for saving him. But what truly surprised her were the slight changes in Terren. He was noticeably nicer compared to his usual moodiness and attitude, for Veronica had saved his life several times by now.

As such, he and Veronica had grown a friendship without either of them realizing it. Henceforth, they—that is to say, Veronica, Terren, and Eco—felt free to share information. Specifically, about Veronica's conversation with Wayloc.

As for Veronica herself, her distrust had lessened slightly. Wayloc seemed kind enough if a bit strict. Terren had recently changed for the better, and Eco had always been kind, in general.

"I've heard of some magic that can keep a person alive," Eco continued while kicking the charred wood from the fire out of the cave. He had finished packing first. "Maybe that's how he's alive." Terren laughed.

"I don't think that would matter, seeing as Mendelo's surely dead. You can't keep him alive if he's dead. He should look like that wood. In fact, he should be dust!"

"Oh, are we calling him Mendelo now?" Eco said sarcastically. "I don't recall you ever mentioning him before, not even by 'the mage.'"

Terren let out a sound that, if it was a little bit louder, would have been a grumble. Veronica and he had already packed all their things, too, and they were waiting for Wayloc to be done. (Apparently, he had lived in the area for a long time, giving him enough time to make himself his own comfortable objects. Naturally, having a hundred handmade pillows doesn't make packing easier.)

"By the way, Eco," Veronica said, remembering something. "How did you do that spike thing with your finger?"

"Oh, that. Well, my species has the peculiar ability to extend our bones. If I wanted, I could transform myself into a horrifying bone monster. Of course, that would be unbearably painful. But, when my race ages, they become immune to the pain. Handy. And once that happens, I'll probably get an edge in fighting."

"Probably," replied Terren.

"If you're not packed, sixty-five times more training in the afternoon." Wayloc walked into the cave. "Oh, good. Eco, why are there dented logs outside? Never mind. Transportation time."

He heaved a heavy sack into a pile with the others' sacks. He said quietly, "Quavikh." A glowing white portal appeared under the sacks, making them fall in. "Your turn. Fallus. You first."

Terren learned the hard way that Wayloc's feelings toward him changed no more than the snow outside the cave. He had jumped in, and Veronica saw that Terren skated on the ground on his rear end that he was running out of sight of the portal in pain.

"Oh, right, I need to rotate the portal. Oops."

11

LORE

THE GIRL WOULD PAY.

Mendelo strolled his office in the Phobia, the tallest tower in all of Nite. Of course, that didn't say much. Nite had been abandoned for more than a century.

He stopped in front of a large glass case and stared at the thing inside, a long, sharp sword made of the fang of a krohla, a giant, extremely venom species of dragon. It was gray, and it looked like stone, but it was much harder. It was around four feet in length, with intricate engravings. Oh, how he longed to use it one day. But there was no one he hated enough to use it on.

The mage walked away, followed by Morgrim and Spectre. Mendelo sat down on his chair and placed his hand on the table. The other hand was absentmindedly stroking Morgrim.

He opened a book on the table and read a page silently. If all went well, the plan would go correctly.

An omnispectre entered the room silently. Mendelo looked up. "What is it?" he asked the omnispectre.

"The Magistrate wishes to see you."

"Fine, fine!" the mage said irritably. "I'll be there." The omnispectre left the room, leaving a trail of black mist.

After the omnispectre left, Mendelo made a motion with his hand to tell his pets to stay. Mendelo walked out into the hall of the castle. Each brick was a dark purple and gray. He came across a pair of massive, obsidian doors and pushed them open with extreme force. The doors cracked where they collided with the wall.

"What is it, Magistrate?!"

The room was large, and a line of omnispectres led up to a black marble throne dotted with precious gems. From the throne, a voice rang out, deep and raspy. "Mendelo…"

He gritted his teeth under his cloak.

"Leave us," the Magistrate said to his minions. The omnispectres obediently dissolved into the ground.

"You said that your pets would help you in the search."

"Oh, they will. I knew that they'd find the tracker eventually. I just needed enough time to summon my two best trackers from the dead." This was a lie. Morgrim and Spectre were not good trackers. In fact, Mendelo hadn't even summoned them from the dead. They never existed, all Mendelo had to do was corrupt two animals with a simple curse, then teleport them to the spot. True necromancy took hours to complete. He had counted on Wayloc's goodie-two-shoes-ness, for he would have never learned the dark art, even if it had brought him back to life. He didn't reveal that the two beasts were fakes to anyone, however. If people thought he was nostalgic, they would have sympathy with him, and therefore weakening them. And the less energy he had to use in a fight, the better.

"Hmm. But even with your two trackers, both the attacks have failed. And I know the cause."

"Yes, my lord?" "Veronica Korix…" The Magistrate laughed a terrible, hoarse laugh. "It is ironic, is it not? With your history…" Mendelo hissed quietly.

"So, you have new orders…" the Magistrate continued. "You cannot touch any of the other magically powerful beings as long as she lives… Kill her, or you will pay… I helped you when I summoned you from the dead. I can revoke that spell…"

"Understood, my lord."

"Good. You are excused."

Mendelo walked out, fighting to keep the murderous intent from bursting out of him. He pushed the doors open gently and walked out into the hall and back into his quarters. His hands were shaking from compressed rage. *Plans… plans… I need plans to kill them all.*

And the plans began. Scribbles of gruesome spells, of horrific transformations, of the most powerfully evil magic. Finally, he came up with it. A machine to purge all that is good and what stands in bravery. Mendelo chuckled. *Bravery. What a feeble, useless thought. Who needs bravery when you have power? And speaking of power, the Master of Malice would defeat the Magistrate in time. In time, he would be dead, and there would be a new ruler.*

Another omnispectre came in. "The Magistrate orders you to—" Mendelo's anger broke through him. He threw a bolt of purple lightning at the omnispectre's head, and as it collided, the omnispectre smoked and shriveled, then fell, slowly turning to black mist.

"The Magistrate no longer has any control over me, even if he thinks so," Mendelo said quietly to himself. "But he was right about one thing."

It all led up to Veronica Korix. All of it. It was all her fault. And he would make her pay dearly. With her life.

The plan was perfect. Almost completely free of issues. But, just in case, he had a backup plan.

He walked in front of the glass case once more. Mendelo pulled off the glass top and touched the hilt of the blade. The Sword of Corruption held terrible power. And he knew, at last, who he was going to use it on.

12

ALL IN FAVOR OF DYING

THE DESERT NIGHTS WERE EVEN more blisteringly hot than the days. Wayloc had set up a tent for the group to share. The new sleeping bags were made for cold days, and Wayloc refused to make them lighter. "You'll sweat off a few pounds," he reasoned.

It seemed that Veronica's eyes wanted to be anyone's but hers during sleep.

Veronica saw through Mendelo's eyes once more. His hands were over his head, and he was shaking. Not with tears. He had not cried in centuries. Crying was for the weak. He was laughing.

"You say that I am doomed?" he breathed to something out of view. "Cursed, am I?"

"You… find the information… humorous…?" groaned a dry, tired voice. "You have cursed yourself, or, rather, the Magistrate has cursed it for you…"

"Impossible…" Mendelo's voice came out as a hiss. The voice gave a wheezing chuckle.

"Think what... you must..."

"And what of"—the humor in his voice vanished— "the thing we discussed."

"As to that... I have... no idea." The voice groaned.

"Oh, walk it off," Mendelo snapped. "What of the presence!?"

"Not a clue..." he coughed.

"I am sure that... someone... Wayloc, maybe, is seeing what I am seeing."

The voice laughed and coughed. "I doubt... you'll ever find out..."

"How dare you!" Mendelo got up and walked toward the voice. He lit his staff with purple light. Revealed by the light was a *wooden man*, strapped to a vertical table.

"I underestimated you, Shaman! You are not just the foolish old Rebellion leader I thought you were! You are a trickster! A magician if you will. Well, I think we should make this *magician* reveal his secrets!"

Mendelo pointed his staff at Shaman's forehead and whispered, "I'm going to enjoy watching you suffer. Nagva!"

Miniature bolts of lightning sprouted out of the staff, wrapping around Shaman's head, sending up sparks. Shaman writhed in his bonds. After a few seconds, Mendelo pulled back the staff from his forehead. "Your pain reminds me. You wondered why I cannot die?" Shaman shuddered. "I'll show you why."

He took off his hood. And Shaman screamed.

Veronica woke up.

"Let me get this straight," Wayloc said. "Shaman has been taken to the Phobia, a literal nightmare tower, and is being tortured for information?"

"That's what the tower's called? Yeah, that's basically it," Veronica confirmed. They all had listened to what she could recall of her dream. Wayloc looked troubled. Terren, disturbed. Eco, terrified. She had expected that. Of what she could infer, Eco was Shaman's trainee, and he seemed to look up to him.

"This is bad. This is very, very bad. Shaman was a major leader of the Rebellion. We've been saving a spot for him in the Rebellion, and now that he might not come back…"

"He will," Veronica said. "Shaman seems smart. But it would be impossible to attack Mendelo head on without, well…"

"Getting decapitated?" Terren provided.

Veronica nodded. "Yeah. Getting decapitated."

"Well, I think we should go to that… nightmare tower thing," said Eco, a surprise for everyone. Eco was a bit of a coward. A thoughtful, smart coward but still, a coward.

"And why the klobtra would we do that?" Wayloc said. "We know going there is suicide."

"And what if it isn't?" Eco snapped. "Shaman was a great teacher and a great friend. Shouldn't we save him from whatever horrible torture he's being subjected to?"

There was a moment of silence. Then Terren said, "I'm with you. Shaman seemed like a nice man."

Wayloc nodded solemnly. They all looked at Veronica. She trusted Shaman now. If he was a spy for the Magistrate, he wouldn't have been tortured.

"Fine. *Fine.* We're all going to be destroyed anyway. All in favor of dying?" Veronica said.

All of them said, in near-perfect unison, "Aye."

The journey took days. As far as I know, the trip was extremely uneventful. So I'll skip to the part where they reached Nite.

"We're nearly there," Wayloc said. They were at the edge of Nite. Veronica thought the entire thing was depressing and clearly radiated fear and evil. The lands were made of sharp hills of black sand. No other features. Except for a massive obsidian tower in the distance. That was noticeable.

"Yeah, I noticed."

"It's going to be a long rest of the walk. However, a teleportation spell will do."

Wayloc closed his eyes, then muttered, "Quavikh." The next moment, they were standing at the gates of the Phobia. The omnispectres guarding the gates were stunned, but they were coming out of their shock. Veronica heaved her sword and gave a soft sigh.

"Just know that you guys voted for this. If I die, I'm going to kill you!"

13

FALLEN MAGIC

THEY HAD TO FIGHT A small fleet of omnispectres. The two omni-spectres had called for backup. The only way to describe it: STAB, STAB, SLASHY-SLASH, SQUISH, *BOOM!* After the battle, they went to the side of the building.

They all decided not to do a human ladder. So, they would use another method.

"I'll climb up the tower with my sword. When I'm up there, I'll bring you up."

They all nodded in general agreement. Veronica thrust her sword in the wall, then climbed on top of her sword, which was firmly wedged in there, then swiftly pulled out her sword from under her and put it into the wall again. Then she repeated the step until she could see through the window of the tower. Before she could pull the others up, however, she saw something that caught her eye.

Mendelo was still torturing Shaman with lightning. His screams were quiet. Mendelo was laughing.

"Hm. It seems that, even after days, I cannot get you to talk. I have no use for you."

He walked to the other side of the room and pulled a white sword out of a cabinet. Veronica had a vague idea of what he was going to do with it. She found a large rock and was ready to throw it. Mendelo was preparing to thrust the sword into Shaman's face. Veronica threw the rock at the sword. The sword was knocked back. Mendelo turned quickly, but not quickly enough.

"Die, you bihk!" Veronica drove the sword into Mendelo's face. The tip of the sword came out the other end.

"Ooh, nice move." Mendelo's hands clasped the sword and pushed it out of his own head, letting it drop to the floor. Veronica then picked it up. "It's just a shame it didn't work. Right through the eye."

Veronica froze in horror as Mendelo grabbed his staff. Shaman called, "Get out of here! I am not worth—"

"Shut it!" Mendelo said in annoyance, glancing at Shaman. Veronica used the distraction to aim at Mendelo's staff. The staff did not break.

"You have nerve coming here!" Mendelo cried as he swung his staff.

Veronica blocked.

"Yeah, I do," Veronica said as she parried several attacks. "What's your point?"

"My point! I don't think I need a point. I'll kill you anyway!" Then Veronica had an idea. She drove her sword sideways, instead of into Mendelo's undefended chest. A light clinking noise was heard.

"Ha! You missed!"

"Did I?"

Shaman was rubbing his wrists, free of his chains. He looked at Mendelo. "Ah, that's better."

It was easily the most powerful fight seen in years.

A green cloak seemed to shimmer into existence around Shaman's shoulders, his cape flowing, his hood fluttering. His wooden form seemed to turn slowly into green light as he floated up. A staff materialized in his hands, and he pointed it at Mendelo. Veronica ducked, faintly hearing the others' cries from down below, as the two mages flew into combat.

"Oh, nice cape!" Mendelo heaved a fireball at Shaman, who summoned a glowing green shield. He yelled, "Tlik!"

The shield hovered toward Mendelo, trying to crush him into the wall, but Mendelo got out his staff, shouted, "Tilta!" His staff turned into a spear, which he used to pierce the shield. He ducked and grabbed the Sword of Corruption. He urged the spear to be a shield of white stone.

Purple smoke swirled around Mendelo as a protective cover. His purple hood fluttered off, though Veronica couldn't see his head. Fireball after fireball launched toward Mendelo but no avail. Mendelo laughed. His voice was clear and sharp, rather than muffled and raspy. (His hood might have disguised his voice.)

Shaman threw not a fireball, but a ball of ice. The smoke turned solid, and Mendelo fell to the ground. The solid smoke blew up, and Mendelo, his hood back on, walked out of the wreckage. He threw down his sword and his shield turned back into a spear. He jumped into the air, preparing to spear Shaman, who was undefended.

Time seemed to slow down. Veronica knew what was going to happen. The others were just outside the window, climbing. Eco's eyes were visible through the window, wide and petrified.

The spear was in Shaman's chest, sinking in. Mendelo laughed. Green blood was dripping out of a chasm in the tree man's chest. He dropped to his knees.

"Ahh…" Shaman groaned. He clawed at his chest and gave one final, shuddering breath. Shaman fell to the floor, his arm bent in an odd angle. The green light in his eyes flickered, then went out. Shaman was gone.

14

MENDELO'S REQUEST

MENDELO NUDGED SHAMAN'S BODY WITH his foot. "Ugh, this takes up too much space in my office. Not nice décor. Perhaps I can use it for firewood?" Mendelo turned to where Veronica was. "But first, I need to take care of something."

Eco leaped out of the window and landed on the dark floor, his eyes once again wide, but occupied with murderous intent. Mendelo waved his hand before he could do anything, and he froze in place, his eyes darting everywhere, half-way through a run. He looked back at Veronica, raised his staff, and the jewel on the top glowed purple. Then she drifted into unconsciousness.

"I see you are awake," said Mendelo.

Veronica was in Mendelo's office. Unchained. And Mendelo was there, too. No one else.

The office itself was a black-walled room with a gray brick floor. There were some closets, some cabinets, some desks, and some cases, all made of dark wood or metal. Inside the cases were weapons and gruesome assortments of animal bones. In a sense, it was a nice office, in a rustic sort of way. But Veronica wasn't going to let Mendelo know that.

"Murderer!" Veronica ran at him, and he sidestepped.

"You interest me, Veronica Korix. I know that you have the unnatural ability to see into my mind."

"I'll kill you!" Veronica shouted though she was paying full attention.

"Yeah, death seems a bit unpleasant to me."

Veronica tried to land a punch at Mendelo, but an invisible wall prevented the impact.

"You cannot harm me," he said, amused.

"Fine," Veronica consented. She dropped her sword hand. Then she tried to kick Mendelo in the chest. It didn't work.

"Hm. Good try, though."

Veronica fell silent.

"Ahem, as I was saying, there seems to be a mental connection, or bridge, between our two psyches. And only you can cross it. I trust that you did not mean for this to happen. You would never be able to do it consciously. I know, of course, why *I* cannot see into your mind."

"And why is that?"

"Because… well, that's a matter for another time. Aside from that, I've been interested in you, Veronica Korix. You remind me of how I was, long ago. Even vaguely in appearance. You also remind me of…" Mendelo paused before continuing. "Like me, you were reckless, yet intelligent. Like me, you wield immense magical power. Like me, you are unafraid of death."

Veronica gritted her teeth. "I'm no—"

"Nothing like me. I thought you'd say that. Especially after Shaman's death. And no, I haven't burned his corpse like I said I would. It's safe in the Magistrate's throne room, being used to traumatize your friends. As I was saying, you are everything like me."

"No. I'm not."

"Well, no, now that I think about it I suppose that isn't true. Not *everything* like me. But alike, nonetheless." He started to loosen his hood. "Both users of magic, though you don't believe so, both, at our hearts, power-hungry, and both human." He paused. "Well… I suppose you are. Me, no longer. I am barely human. I am not held together by flesh and bone, the only thing that holds me up is *myself! Me, myself,* and my *magic.*"

"Why would you need to do that?" Veronica asked in a shaky voice.

Mendelo gave a raspy laugh. "See for yourself." He took off his hood, and Veronica let out a shuddering gasp. What she saw was horrible. His face had no skin, no flesh. His eye sockets were cruel and unblinking. His hard, white jaw stretched into an unnerving grin. Mendelo's head was a skull. All bone.

"Cliché, I know. Ninety percent of all dark mages in pop culture have skulls for faces. Your friend Eco tried to punch me in the head. His hand almost broke. Your sword went through my eye socket. Ring any bells?" He pulled back on his hood. "You see, long ago, I died. Long before you were born, mind you, long before even this world was remade! And I didn't just die, I was murdered! But one day, *one day,* I was brought back. Sadly, the Magistrate is terrible at necromancy, and I had to come back as *this.* But I was fine with it if I lived. And it's a great scare tactic. Wayloc, however, was brought back before me, by someone much better at necromancy, I imagine…"

"Now back to the deal," Mendelo said to a horror-stricken Veronica. "Join forces with me, and you will learn magical powers you could have never imagined. Refuse to join forces and…"

"Let me guess, you kill me."

"Indeed! I wonder how you guessed. Now, decide, it should not be so hard."

Veronica's mind was still in turmoil, but now it was forced to decide. Mendelo was evil and, there was no denying it, insane. But if he could bring Shaman back…

No. No chance she was siding with Shaman's killer. Her only hope was to lie to Mendelo, assuming magic didn't allow you to read minds, which she hoped it wouldn't.

"All I ask for in return is your help in the Magistrate's death."

"I thought you were—"

"I am not the Magistrate's servant! The Magistrate is a simple-minded idiot, a brute, if you will! I do not serve fools."

"Mmm… what are you going to do after?"

"I plan to summon an… apparition… that will help me change the world for the *better*."

Veronica thought about it for a minute, or she pretended to, anyway. Then she smirked. "Fine," she said. "If you kill the Magistrate and bring back Shaman, you have a deal."

Mendelo took off his glove, revealing his bony hand. "Let's shake on it."

"Let's not."

15

THE THRONE OF FEAR

THE THRONE WAS OBSIDIAN AND crested with purple and red jewels. It was surrounded by omnispectres on both sides. And on it sat a shadowy figure, sure to be the doom of Veronica. Hidden by darkness, his presence dampened any hope for life.

Veronica was led, hands pinned to her back, into the clean, black-bricked room. The walls were polished. Omnispectres were covered with dark armor and wielded long spears. The place radiated fear, despair, and evil. And, naturally, Mendelo and the Magistrate were smack in the middle of it.

The guards holding them stopped just before the steps to the throne. And then a voice, a deep, raspy, ominous voice, echoed through the room, and it seemed, the world.

"Veronica Korix, you have been caught directly associating and working with the Rebellion, a heinous crime."

Veronica gave a nervous laugh. (Literally the worst thing she could have done at the time.) "I wouldn't say heinous, per se…"

The Sword of Corruption was a centimeter from her throat. "May I destroy her?" Mendelo inquired of his master.

"Not yet."

Mendelo lowered his sword and looked back at Veronica. His eye socket twitched, as if he was trying to wink, but not quite managing it. Little did he know, he needn't have winked at all. Veronica would not be following the plan.

The Magistrate continued. "Of course, there is another crime to which you have been accused: the death of General Dusk, an omnispectre you murdered. The death has been repaid, however, in the form of your friend Shaman."

An omnispectre entered the room through a separate door, dragging Shaman's body carelessly. It was dropped on the floor near the Magistrate.

"His corpse has been used to torture your friends, as well. It's ironic how much the dead has an impact on the living."

Omnispectres brought Wayloc, Eco, and Terren through the same door Shaman came through. Wayloc was covered in a metal sarcophagus with eye holes, to keep in his magic. Eco was shaking, his pupils dilated in terror. Terren wasn't too much better.

"Ah, ah, I remember something," the Magistrate said. "The dead having an impact on the living. That is appropriate in your case, Veronica Korix."

"What do you mean?"

"Your mother was in the Rebellion."

Veronica had felt a surprising number of emotions in this tower. But this piece of information, this one fact about her past she didn't know hit her the most. Time slowed. Her breathing quickened. Too many pieces fell together at once.

"Marian Korix. A great warrior. I sent Mendelo to her cabin to destroy her if I remember correctly."

Shock slowly turned to realization. Veronica felt a tingling sensation in her hands, though her focus was not on it at that very moment. The Magistrate got up out of his chair. "She must have hidden you before her death."

Veronica's realization turned to rage. The sensation became ten times more powerful. Mendelo was shaking his head. His plan was crashing around his skull. The Magistrate put one foot out into the open. It was made of ink and shadows, exactly like an omnispectre. "Poor, orphan Veronica Korix, having to live by herself for so long."

Veronica was shaking with something past rage, now. The sensation was strong now. The Magistrate came out into the open, a large omnispectre with a light-purple circle mask, wielding a massive black axe.

"Goodbye…" He heaved the axe.

And Veronica exploded. Quite literally. Some pens might write that she didn't really explode, but, to the omnispectres, it sure looked like it. She let out a huge burst of glowing white energy, which vaporized the omnispectres pinning hers, Eco's, and Terren's arms.

The Magistrate's mask cracked vertically and opened in tune with a high shriek. "Attack!"

At that moment, pandemonium reigned. A spear flew past Veronica's ear, and she knew that was her cue to leave. "Come on!" she yelled to the others. Terren got out of his state and pushed Eco with him, who was shivering and scared. "What about Wayloc?"

Terren shrugged, but then Veronica remembered something under the pressure of the closing army. Veronica held out her hand and said, "Vox!" A spark flew out of her palm.

"Stroke your palm when you do it, now!" Terren said. The army was getting closer, their spears held forward.

Veronica stroked her palm downward and repeated the phrase. For the first time, a fireball burst out of her palm, burning a hole through Wayloc's metal prison. His hand groped for a moment, then his prison exploded, sending shards of metal everywhere and knocking the omni-spectres back.

"Ah," Wayloc cried, half-annoyed, half-angry. "Now, let's kill a ton of blood-thirsty monsters! Shouldn't be too hard!"

16

THE RAIN

THE BATTLE WAS OVER QUICKLY. Veronica dodged spears left and right while occasionally shooting fireballs. Wayloc did much of the same. Terren, his sword gone, hit people mostly. And Eco was being shielded by everyone else, in shock.

The battle didn't get any better when Mendelo's pets joined the fray. However, Terren wrestled them to the ground, an impressive feat for an unarmed man.

Soon, the army was nearly gone. The omnispectres had almost completely fled. But most were dead at the hands of Veronica, Terren, and Wayloc. Super dead. The pets were unconscious. Now two opponents remained, and they were the worst of them all.

The Magistrate launched himself into the air and cracked the floor under him on landing. The axe rematerialized in his hands, two times longer than before, and five times as deadly. An execution axe. He raised his palm, and a beam of deadly light narrowly missed Veronica's head. Wayloc jumped forward and encased the Magistrate's hand in light.

"Get off!" the Magistrate yelled.

"Run!" Wayloc shouted to them. He opened a portal a few feet away. "I'll be there! Just a moment! It's not as if trapping a demon god-king is hard!"

Veronica and the others started to run, but the Sword of Corruption flew past her, brushing her hair but narrowly missed her face. The hair that the sword brushed turned gray. (This later made her well known, as the few strands that were gray added to her noticeability and mystique.)

She turned to see Mendelo standing, his hood fluttering, his teeth bared under the shadow of his cloak. "Shaman will never live again, Veronica Korix, and it's your fault!"

"Well, you didn't expect me to work with *you*? With your creepy messed-up excuse of a face?!"

"*Rraagh!*" Mendelo flew at Veronica, but she dodged and ran with the others to the portal. Mendelo slammed into the opposite wall and fell, stunned.

"Tlik!" Veronica yelled, raising her hand at the Magistrate, and he smashed into the steps of the throne, giving Wayloc time to run to the portal with the others. Eco, Terren, and Wayloc jumped into the swirling, glowing portal. Veronica ran for Shaman's corpse and dragged it back.

"So long, bihks!" Veronica yelled before she jumped in herself, taking Shaman's body with her. The portal closed behind her.

The group was standing in a small, mossy clearing, not like that in the first clearing, for it was neither beautiful nor good smelling. Eco had gotten over his terrible state and was walking in circles, his eyes wide. Occasionally, he gave a small shiver.

Terren was sitting on a log, his head in his hands, shaking his head in denial, and Wayloc stood solemnly next to Shaman's body, propped up against a tree.

It had started to rain. After what seemed like an eternity, Eco turned to Veronica. "What did he mean?" Eco asked quietly. "'Shaman will never live again, and it's your fault.' What did Mendelo mean?"

Veronica looked down and thought whether she should tell him the truth. Eco and the others deserved the information. Especially Eco. To him, Shaman was a father figure, rather than a teacher. And, at last, Veronica finally trusted him.

"Before we were in the throne room, Mendelo and I talked. He said if I helped him overthrow the Magistrate, he'd bring… he'd bring Shaman back."

Eco turned. His face was filled with an eerie darkness. He paused, leaving a painful silence. The individual vines in his arms seemed to tremble slightly. "He could have been brought back…"

Then raging green flames sparked into existence in the hollow on Eco's plant-shaped head, unperturbed by the rain. He turned swiftly to Veronica. His eyes were bright white, he was much taller, and his arms and legs were slender, ending in long, thin claws. It was as if the *bones* were extending. Terren and Wayloc shot into fighting positions as Eco pinned Veronica to a nearby tree. "You could have brought him back!" Eco hissed. "He could have been alive if you had just… had just…"

Eco slackened his grip. The flame in his head shrank with the rest of his body. His eyes became normal. He let go and backed away a few steps. The drops of rain slid down his face in sync with the tears. Wayloc went over to him and put his hand on his shoulder in a fatherly fashion. Veronica left the clearing.

17

PAST AND PRESENT

VERONICA WAS SITTING ON A log by the creek, some way away from the clearing, thinking. Eco had always seemed so polite, but, for now, he was accusatory. Had Veronica done the right thing, not trusting Mendelo? Mendelo was thinking the opposite. She knew that because of that "bridge between their psyches". Had *he* chosen correctly in trusting Veronica?

What would have happened if she had followed Mendelo? The Magistrate would be dead. Shaman would be alive. *Mendelo couldn't be any worse a ruler than the Magistrate, right?* Yes. Yes, he could.

Terren stumbled through the woods behind her, grumbling from his many splinters. "You know, I think you're on the right path. Distrusting Mendelo to honor the deal, I mean. Wayloc doesn't think he would have honored the deal, either."

"I know. Eco's just stressed, I think. In shock."

"Yeah…" Terren said. "May I?"

"Sure."

Terren sat down on the log.

"Ew, you smell," Veronica pointed out, noticing a truly awful smell.

"Well, you aren't any better! Like you, I haven't had a change of clothes for nearly a week. I haven't had a decent *shower,* either." He gestured to his ragged clothes covered with thin pieces of stray armor and to her sand-colored cloak, covered in mud and some armor.

"Didn't notice that. Must have been all the excitement." They sat in silence for a moment, staring at the flowing water of the creek. Then Terren brought up a question.

"What's your story?" he asked.

Veronica looked at him quizzically.

"I mean, the Magistrate mentioned your mom, and I just wondered..."

Veronica looked solemn and a bit annoyed.

"I still have my sword. Not afraid to use it, you know."

Then she sighed and looked down. "My mom died when I was young. My dad, even sooner. You know why she's dead, of course. After that, not much. Lianthorn, an elf, took partial care of me, but I mostly took care of myself. Joined a bounty hunter school at age ten, graduated at sixteen. Then I hunted." She shook her head. "Never missed having parents. Never will." But she knew that this was not true, and she knew that Terren knew it, too.

She turned her head to Terren again. "What about you? Who was that woman whose house you were hiding in the day I beat you up?"

"That was my cousin, Flavia. Bihk. And a true idiot. Thought she would be fined or arrested or something if she gave me housing. Thought it would save money to make holes instead of stairs, and she could get bouncy shoes to get up. What if she'd lost her shoes? She'd be dead. Her food supply is on the second floor."

"Certainly, a dummy."

"Yeah. My parents both died when I was young, so I was brought up by my grandparents. When they went, I was eighteen—technically an adult. Then, I stole a sword and rebelled against the Magistrate."

"Flavia's not the only idiot, then."

Terren smiled ever so slightly. "Eco should have calmed down by now. I'll check." Terren left.

That was better. For some reason. Veronica was now in a surprisingly calm mood. And in a thoughtful one. How would they recover from this blow? And how could they get back up again? How did generals in armies do it? *Ah. That's how. A bit unconventional, but...*

Eco was sitting on a log. He looked calmer than last time. He was also surrounded by Wayloc and Terren, who weren't mad, but not exactly cheery either. The moment Veronica entered the clearing, Eco looked up. His eyes were slightly red. "What do you want?"

Veronica ignored this comment and stood upon a tree stump, then cleared her throat. Everyone looked, even Eco.

"I know we're in a tough situation, with… one thing or another," Veronica said. "You probably think we're way in over our heads. We probably have no chance against the Magistrate's massive army of omnispectres."

"The Magistrate has armies like the one we faced in every country," Wayloc added. "And he can compile them at any second."

"Yeah. For all we know, they could be tracking us. And Mendelo is planning something. And it can't be good." Veronica took a deep breath. "But if he's planning something, we will, too. If the Magistrate's gathering his army, we're getting the Rebellion, and you know why?" She inhaled slightly. "Because the Magistrate's a bihk!" she said, lamely.

The word "bihk" echoed throughout the forest. None of the others spoke for a moment. There was an awkward silence.

Then Eco stood up. "That… was the stupidest thing I've ever heard. I'm in. No more running."

18

FINALLY, A REAL REBELLION

AFTER SHAMAN'S BURIAL, TRAINING BEGAN. The next few days were devoted to it. Now that Veronica had finally unlocked her powers, she was a much better disciple.

"Can't I just do the thing I did at the Phobia?" she asked Wayloc. "Vaporize 'em all?"

"No. That burst of energy was just from the magic being unlocked after such a long time. It had time for it to grow. Emotional magic, you know. Very strong, but it's not nearly as strong as that. And you can't just 'vox' everyone again like last time. I'd be surprised if you weren't completely drained."

It was true. Veronica had felt very tired after last night and had a very good sleep. "Magic is all about strategy. What spell should you use in a battle? Which spells will drain your energy, and if they're worth the risk? The vox spell doesn't drain too much if you only say it once. If you are to use it, wait a bit—ten seconds, at least."

"What spells use the least energy?"

"Three. Breeze spell, eye irritation spell, and face irritation spell. But only the breeze and face irritation spells are useful, as neither the Magistrate nor omnispectres nor Mendelo have eyes. The other two spells are *mak*, breeze, and *pov*, face irritation."

"Hm. What's eyes? You know, just in case."

"Oh, well. It's *nor*."

"Oh, okay. I'll test it. *Nor!*"

Wayloc stumbled back, rubbing his eyes. "Why, oh, why?" he half-sobbed. Tears spewed from his eyes. "I'm gonna get you for this! Why…"

"I'll… just leave you there," Veronica whispered. "You have fun with that. I-I'm backing away now. Backing away…"

Veronica observed Terren's training as well. Wayloc had decreed that it would take a few more years for his magic to come out. He apparently could only channel magic through objects.

"Maybe you could wear something magical to channel magic *through*. Perhaps gloves. But it shall only work if you make it yourself. Try metal. The magic should make it much lighter."

"How does that work?"

"No clue. Don't question it. There's a reason they call it magic, you know. It makes no sense."

"I think I know what I'm gonna do…"

Eco didn't need training. Wayloc had trusted him with the best blade he had, a kindrosword. "It's a very hard metal, perfect for facing multiple enemies at once and for throwing."

Eco held it with awe, looking at its green blade and blue hilt, then, a split second later, threw it at a wooden dummy on the other side of the clearing. It drove into the dummy's forehead and out of the back of its head, where it stuck into a tree.

"You're a good shot," Wayloc said, surprised. Eco had been training endlessly and with a certain power ever since Veronica's speech. Apparently, it worked.

On the final day, everyone gathered in the middle of the clearing except Terren, who had said it would be a few minutes. "Terren is not here yet, so I suppose we must start without him. I decided for you to become fully fledged Rebellion soldiers. And with it, you need these." Wayloc handed out watches that had black screens on them. "Silent communication devices. A bit old but useful. Only the wearer can hear it."

Veronica fitted on hers and noticed something. "There's one left for... oh, there you are."

Terren rushed into the clearing and immediately put on the device. He seemed to know these were devices already.

"Sorry, just made some other touches to... well, now that we have the devices, what's the plan?"

"Veronica?" Eco asked. "You have any?" They all looked expectantly at her. Veronica inwardly congratulated herself on her leadership skills.

"Okay. Here's the plan."

19

SIEGE

THIS DEMON WOULD HELP. HE had been planning it for months. Veronica Korix was only a backup plan to defeat the Magistrate. But the demon would. *If only I could summon it!*

"*Raa!*" Mendelo swiped the books off the desk. Mendelo knew everything but one rune to summon the beast. *The Magistrate already suspects me. It's only a matter of time...*

If he summoned the demon, it could kill the Magistrate. Then he could return to his true mission, to find...

Mendelo wished dearly to kill Veronica Korix, who had ruined the plan. If she had just played along...

What he wouldn't give to find her and destroy her. What he wouldn't give to rule the world. What he wouldn't give to...

Mendelo saw through Veronica's eyes for the first time. She was standing alone at the gates of the Phobia.

Mendelo's eyes flashed back. He breathed heavily. She was at the gates. Alone. Veronica Korix had a plan. Absentmindedly, Mendelo picked up a book from the floor and started flipping through pages. Then something caught his eye. The rune. It was on the page. He had found it.

Omnispectres brought Veronica in, all according to plan.

"There's a new general," one omnispectre said to his brother. "A human one."

"Wonder what he does to the prisoner," the other said, and they both grinned horribly. She was inside the large, clean, black hall. At this time, Eco would be destroying all other guard omnispectres, and Wayloc would be leading all the other Rebellion members to surround the tower.

The omnispectres stopped. A man walked down the hall toward them. He had black armor from head to toes and a flowing black cape. He had two glowing yellow visors, one above the other. He held a familiar golden sword. "Please," one omnispectre said, "do the honors."

The man raised his sword. It opened, revealing a yellow light. In a few seconds, the omnispectres at Veronica's either side exploded with two sharp blasts. "Thanks, General Fallus."

"Ha, ha." Terren laughed sarcastically. He took off his helmet. "Nice job with the infiltration. Where's Eco?"

"Right here." Eco was barely noticeable until he spoke. He jumped down from the other floor. He was carrying the blue and green kindrosword. "The left wing and the fourth floor are clear. Wayloc should have infiltrated the tower by now."

"The Magistrate knows we've infiltrated the tower," Terren added. "And he's gonna face us head on in the center of the tower."

"Good, then we can face him head on, as well. Keep eliminating the leftover omnispectres. The fewer enemies, the better."

Eco went into a separate hall, Terren in another, and Veronica walked wearily forward. She opened a door slowly to see four omnispectres turned the other way. She raised her palm, pressed her finger to the back of her hand, and hissed, "Vip."

The omnispectres didn't notice that they could no longer talk or call for help.

Veronica waited three seconds, then said, "Vivikh."

Five fireballs zoomed toward the omnispectres just as they turned. They all dissolved into black mist without a sound. The room was otherwise empty. Terrible portraits of the Magistrate's omnispectre ancestors looked down at her unnervingly.

Then, out of nowhere, Morgrim tackled her from behind, while Spectre appeared in front, preparing to burn her face off. She grabbed Morgrim off her back and threw it at Spectre, extinguishing the fire in its throat. Morgrim barfed ice spikes at her face. Veronica melted them with a well-timed "vox."

She grabbed Morgrim while he was still stunned and held him up just as Spectre shot flames at her. Then the evil dog fell, nearly dead from its ally's flames. Spectre was stunned at the fall of its compatriot, then, with a flurry of rage, flew up into the air and vomited fire spikes once more. "Vexi!" Veronica yelled. The fire spikes dissolved in midair. "Now, presenting the trilogy of pain! Nor! Mak! Pov!"

The cat howled in pain. First, its eyes watered, then its face started sweating, then it seemed the effects were pushed a little deeper under its skin. It was blind now. Veronica kicked it into the wall, and it crumpled, unconscious. Veronica walked out of the room.

20

THE REBELLION'S LAST STAND

THE ROOM WAS COMPLETELY SILENT. One side of the room, led by the Magistrate, was mostly just omnispectres. Mendelo was at his side. On the other side were a variety of humans, elves, and other creatures, led by Wayloc. Veronica was silently walking, making sure she was not heard, as she snuck behind the opposing ranks.

"It will be a massive victory to kill all the best Rebellion members at once," the Magistrate called across the room.

"It will be one for us, as well!" Wayloc called. "Once we kill you, the world will be free." *Oh, save us from your banter,* Veronica thought.

"You think so?"

"I know so. Why don't you see for yourself?" Veronica knew this was her cue. She hid in the crowd of omnispectres and whirled around her sword, taking out seven omnispectres.

Startled, the Magistrate yelled, "Attack!"

"Charge!" Wayloc called from the other side. The two sides surged forward. Weapons clashed. Screams were heard. Veronica saw Molis, a very old man with goggles and a blaster-proof vest, raise a massive war-hammer to smash opposing omnispectres. Soon there were only two people were not battling: Veronica and Mendelo. Veronica raised her palm and hit Mendelo with a fireball, who dodged.

"Vexi!"

All warmth escaped Veronica, and she didn't like the feeling. Before he could do anything else, Veronica escaped into the ensuing madness. Rebellion peoples' bodies were scattered everywhere, and the same number of omnispectres was dead.

A rain of fire, caused by Mendelo, pelted down on the ground, harming both the Rebellion and the Magistrate's forces. Terren, in his black armor and helmet, ran through the crowd of battling people toward Veronica. "Wayloc's fighting the Magistrate, and he's not doing too great, and I don't know where Eco is. Anything on your end?"

Veronica looked up, and said, "That." She sidestepped as the Sword of Corruption drove into the ground. Mendelo pulled it out of the ground and swung it at Veronica before she could move. *Clang!*

The sword against the kindrosword made an unpleasant ringing sound. Eco pushed him back with his blade and began a glorious duel. Mendelo's hood slid off, revealing his newly cracked skull.

"I'll kill you, even if you're as powerful as your face is ugly!" Mendelo snarled, his bones twisting. Terren and Veronica ducked as an omnispectre flew over their heads.

"You didn't mention that Mendelo was a bonehead!" Terren shouted over the noise. Eco threw his sword into Mendelo's chest, through the ribcage. He jumped on the hilt and kicked Mendelo in the face in midair, grabbing his sword from his chest as Mendelo flew back. Mendelo got up and attempted to slash Eco, who parried. He pushed Mendelo to the ground with his sword. The blade was at his throat.

"You lose," Eco whispered, barely audible through the pandemonium of the battle. Mendelo seemed to look at Eco even if he didn't have eyes.

Mendelo smiled. "No. You lose." He raised his other hand and yelled, "Mak!"

The breeze got into Eco's eyes just long enough for Mendelo to jump up and drive the sword into Eco's shoulder. He screamed in pain. Mendelo pulled the sword out. Green blood dripped down. Mendelo pulled his hood back on. Veronica and Terren rushed forward.

"Oh, gods," Terren said as Veronica looked at his eyes.

"He's still alive," Veronica noted. "But…" The spot where he was bleeding was turning stony gray, and just as hard. And the gray was growing across Eco's right arm.

"Wait." She had remembered the word for delay. "Enbis." The bleeding and the decaying stopped. Eco closed his eyes and went limp. "He's unconscious."

Suddenly, the battle stopped. Veronica pushed her way through the still people and omnispectres. When she got to the front of the crowd, she saw Mendelo, laughing like a madman, gazing at a circle in the ground with peculiar shapes around the edges. To add to the ominous scene, the circle and the runes were glowing purple.

Wayloc raised his staff. "What are you doing, you fool?!"

The Magistrate screeched at the same time as Wayloc. "Mendelo, what are you doing?!"

"Killing you off, that's what!" Mendelo responded. "Both of you!" Then, he started chanting in an ancient tongue. His hood flew off and his eye sockets glowed purple as he floated a few feet off the ground.

The Magistrate ran at him, but a force field of purple energy prevented him from penetrating the edge of the circle.. A glowing portal formed in the circle, and a massive hand made of black smoke rose from it. Then came an arm, then a torso, then a full body appeared, its eyes as purple as Mendelo's. Its mouth was wide in an evil grin, and its head barely scraped the ceiling. It gave a massive intake of breath, then screeched at the horrified crowd.

21

THE SHADOW COLOSSUS

"HA! FINALLY!" MENDELO YELLED WITH delight, his eyes no longer glowing, and he was no longer floating. He had accomplished his goal after so many years. "Beast!"

The monster turned, obviously not flattered by being called "beast."

"Destroy the Magistrate!" He pointed at his former master. He looked at the unresponsive colossus. "Go! Listen to your master!"

The colossus did nothing, staring at Mendelo. "You stupid apparition!" the mage screeched. 'Go, idiotic creature! Go!"

The colossus snarled, raised his fist, and brought it down. Mendelo groaned. "Oh, klobtra."

Boom! The colossus raised his fist from the spot where Mendelo was, and what was now a pile of rubble. It looked at the still crowd, then roared.

"Retreat!" the Magistrate shouted, and his forces retreated from the room, but not before the colossus ate a few. The remaining Rebellion members charged, however. Wayloc shot spells at the beast, while the others shot at the thing with their blasters or poked it with their weapons.

The beast was unphased, and in no time at all, only Wayloc was standing. But then the beast swiped at him, and he was unconscious as well. Terren and Veronica were in a corner, tending to Eco's wounds. Or at least Terren was. Veronica was watching the battle in horror.

"It's gonna tear this place apart!" Veronica whispered.

Once Terren knew that Eco was going to be okay, he got up.

"Agreed. I attack from the bottom, you on the top. We meet in the middle."

They both ran at the beast, but the plan failed immediately. The moment they separated, Terren was swiped out of the way and landed unconscious on the floor. It was all up to her now. She flung out her sword and drove it into the monster's foot. The colossus grunted, then tried to reach to his toes.

Veronica pulled the sword out and broke it in two halves against her knee, making two equally deadly blades. She drove both blades farther into the foot. This time, the colossus screeched. It swatted at Veronica, but she was too quick. She climbed up the colossus, one blade at a time until she was high up at the monster's hip. Then, she let go of one blade and let the other go down the monster, making a huge gash in the leg.

The colossus screeched in pain and fell over, destroying most of the building. Veronica sprinted over to where the monster's enormous head was, then slashed at the monster's face. The monster, probably realizing it had a size disadvantage, shrunk to three times her size, a million times smaller than its last form. It got up, then screeched.

Its legs grew into spider legs, which it used to try to smash Veronica, who expertly adapted to the monster's size. She slashed off one leg, then another, until it opened its mouth and blasted beams of light at her.

"Oh, really?" Veronica exclaimed.

It let out a shriek that sent debris falling. Veronica ran in for an exposed spot on the back, aiming to kill. Then the monster pinned her to the ground with its back legs and turned its torso one hundred eighty degrees to stare at her. It opened its mouth, ready to blast her face off.

Veronica knew she was going to die. But she wasn't going to die without a fight. She couldn't drive her swords through at this angle, but she could…

"Hey!" The colossus stared. "Oh, my gods. Behind you. Look!"

It worked. The monster turned its head.

Veronica raised her right palm and yelled, "Tlik!"

The colossus moved just enough for her to grab her swords and jump into the air.

"Eat metal, bihk!"

The monster fell to its knees, the swords in its chest, both through where the lungs should have been. Then it dissolved into mist, leaving the two swords on the floor where it once was.

Veronica bent down and grabbed her swords. There was an aching pain in her ribs. Then she walked over to Wayloc's unconscious form and shook him awake. He murmured, opened his eyes, then got up.

"It's dead?"

Veronica nodded.

"I think you should probably…" Veronica gestured at the Rebellion members on the floor, some of whom were stirring.

"Yes, but the ceiling's going to collapse. Our priority is to get outside." He raised his hand, then shouted, "Quavikh!"

22

THE END AND THE BEGINNING

THE NEXT FEW DAYS WERE the best the world had seen in centuries. The Magistrate was driven into hiding, his forces disbanded, and his most powerful servant gone. All because of Veronica Korix.

A few days after the battle, Veronica was asked to attend a meeting of governors, and she accepted. The meeting place was in Rellicos City, somewhere she did not want to go to after the mayhem she had caused there only days before. But she accepted anyway.

Rellicos was awfully quiet the day she visited. Everyone was either in the alleys or in their houses. The meeting took place in the tallest building near the plaza. She walked in, took the elevator to the highest floor, and waited.

After a few minutes, the elevator dinged, then opened. Veronica walked into the room, which had a long table surrounded by four chairs. Three of the chairs had well-dressed people in them, and one was empty. For her.

"Hello," one governor said. He was bald, with dark skin and blue eyes. His hands were folded. "Please, sit down."

Once she was seated, she asked the question she had been thinking about all morning. "Why am I here?"

The governors' eyes widened for a moment. The one who had first spoken answered, "Well, it's complicated."

Another governor, a pale woman, cleared her throat. "The Magistrate's disappearance is good for the society and the world. But there's a massive power vacuum. The society might crumble without a leader."

The third governor, a wispy old man, said, "That is why we've come to a decision that will benefit both the society and you."

"We want you to be monarch," the first governor finished. "You can accept the offer or you can decide not to. With you as the ruler, we trust we'll have the time to assemble the other countries' governors."

Veronica had to think. If she accepted, she wouldn't have to do bounty hunting anymore. She could be a better ruler than the Magistrate. But then again, she might be worse. She knew what happened when there was one single ruler. The two ideas clashed in her mind until, at last, she made her decision.

"I have made my final decision." The governors looked at her expectantly. "I choose…"

Far away, in the ruins of the Phobia, a storm was brewing. The rain poured down onto the destroyed black stone. Then, the bricks quivered slightly. It might have been the rain. Or the wind.

But it wasn't.

Then, a single stone brick moved one centimeter. It started to crack. Then, it broke open as a hand, a bony skeleton hand, rose out from under it. Then, a figure pushed itself out of the rubble. It was draped in a tattered purple and black cloak, and it had a skull for a head. The crack on his skull was prominent.

Mendelo growled as he looked at the wreckage of the tower. "All that work... crushed. Centuries of artifacts and magical books... destroyed."

"Veronica Korix. Need to get to Veronica Korix." He pulled the Sword of Corruption out of the stone, broken into two. Then he tossed it into the debris.

He would be better than the Magistrate when he succeeded in his plan. Better than any omnispectre that ever ruled. They ruled with fear and strength. He would rule with intelligence and power.

But before anything, he would find Veronica Korix. He walked across the rubble in the direction of Rellicos City. The raindrops slid off his head. Something had permanently broken inside of him.

The Master of Malice would rise again.